NANCY WARREN

Frosted Shadow

A TONI DIAMOND MYSTERY

ISBN: ebook 978-1-928145-98-1

ISBN: print 978-0-9920780-0-3

Cover Design by Stunning Book Covers

Ambleside Publishing

INTRODUCTION

There's nothing pretty about murder.

Meet Toni Diamond, makeup artist to middle America. She's got a nose for trouble and a passion for solving mysteries. Imagine Columbo in a lavender suit. She never met a woman who wouldn't look better with a little help from the Lady Bianca line of cosmetics. But don't be fooled by appearances. Underneath the fake diamonds and the big hair is a sharp brain and a keen eye that sees the details as well as the funny side of life. When a Lady Bianca sales rep is murdered at the annual convention in Dallas, Toni is the one who notices things that some people, like sexy Detective Luke Marciano, might easily miss. Only someone who understands as much about how to make appearances deceiving could see into the mind of this killer—a murderer who wants to give Toni a permanent makeover. Into a dead woman.

PRAISE FOR THE TONI DIAMOND MYSTERIES

FROSTED SHADOW

"This series is first class. Super intrigue and great characters."

— LINDA

ULTIMATE CONCEALER

"Never a dull moment. Nancy Warren is a true entertainer."

— BELINDA WILSON

MIDNIGHT SHIMMER

"Fantastic from start to finish."

— PATTI SANDERS

A DIAMOND CHOKER FOR CHRISTMAS

"I loved every minute of the book."

— GAIL A. DEMAREE

FROSTED SHADOW

CHAPTER 1

I'm tired of all this nonsense about beauty being only skin-deep. That's deep enough. What do you want, an adorable pancreas?

–Jean Kerr

Some people are born beautiful. Obviously, not that many or cosmetics wouldn't be a multi-billion dollar industry and Toni Diamond wouldn't be giving her rah-rah speech to the new sales recruits for Lady Bianca cosmetics.

"I believe in the power of Lady Bianca makeup, to transform, to inspire, to bring out a new woman," she told the thousand newbie delegates at the national conference in Corvallis, Texas, a suburb of Dallas. They felt the same according to the enthusiastic applause that greeted her.

"I believe in the right of every woman to look her best." While Toni paused to sip water, another tsunami of applause swept the packed ballroom of the convention hotel.

Toni sold Lady Bianca Cosmetics the way old-time preachers sold a revival. With passion, fire, and a healthy dose of fear of the consequences of remaining on the path to ruin.

You committed the sins of smoking, working too hard, eating junk food, drinking too much, or—God forbid—sunbathing, and there would be retribution. Premature aging. Wrinkles. Dull, lifeless skin, eyes with no sparkle. Lips sucked dry of youth and passion.

"We sell the best cosmetics on the market today, and we should be proud of what we do." Toni figured that rebirth of the soul was between a woman and God. But during that gal's time here on earth, Lady Bianca cosmetics could offer the skincare sinner salvation in a five-step regimen followed by a full line of paints, powders, and creams to pretty up that refreshed skin.

"We brighten tired eyes, breathe youth into lifeless lips, dew onto leathered skin. When we are done with a makeover, our customer is *born again*—cosmetically, anyway."

Here she stood, a cosmetics evangelist in her purple power suit sparkling with diamond buttons. There were diamonds on pretty much everything Toni owned, from her sunglasses to her shoes. "Branding" they called it. Every time a woman saw a diamond she wanted that woman to think of Toni Diamond and then consider whether she didn't need a few more cosmetics from her favorite Lady Bianca rep.

"Are you proud to be running your own business? Let me hear you. Are you proud to be empowering women?"

Now the hand-clapping was thunderous. There were some hoots and wolf-whistles thrown into the mix. These gals were pumped. She loved the new recruits, loved their enthusiasm, their hope, and energy. They were the future of the company gazing up at her like sunflowers reaching for the sun.

They were young, middle-aged, and old. They came from all backgrounds, but they had one thing in common. With varying degrees of desperation, these women wanted to make money in the beauty business and they were looking to her to show them how.

Personal success stories were big at the Lady Bianca convention and hers was a pretty good one. Who didn't love a Cinderella-from-the-trailer-park tale? "I remember sitting in this room fifteen years ago. I was a teenaged single mom. Broke, desperate and close to homeless."

Hallelujah.

"My story starts out like a country song. My man done me wrong, left me and the baby, and then the truck died."

Laughter floated up to the stage, but everybody here had her own story, some a lot sadder than Toni's. "The one thing my seventeen-year-old husband left me,"—since she considered the baby all hers and one unexcitingly delivered sperm did not a father make—"was his glitzy last name. In this life you have to take your treasures where you find them. And no feminist on earth was going to stop me trading Plotnik for Diamond.

"Well, me and my fancy last name were picking over the bruised apples at the grocery store one day when a beautifully-dressed woman came up to me and offered me a free makeover." She grinned down at her rapt audience. "I must have looked like I'd been ridden hard and put away wet. You can imagine—" She was interrupted by a scream. Not a *You go girl* holler either, but a heart-pounding scream of panic.

A rustle of apprehension rippled through the crowded room.

"A Lady Bianca rep's been murdered," a woman yelled.

"What?" Toni's voice boomed through the microphone.

Panic swept through those happy sunflowers like a brush fire. Women jumped to their feet and fell over their conference bags, their high-heeled shoes, and each other stampeding for the exits.

"Hey, calm down," she commanded through the microphone.

"Don't panic. This is probably just a crazy rumor. Take your time heading out and show me the Lady Bianca spirit."

Murder? At a conference on beauty, female empowerment, and success? Impossible. But Toni knew she'd been hopelessly upstaged and there was no point continuing for the few remaining women who had the sense to stay in their seats.

When Toni emerged into the main hallway, she was struck by the hushed atmosphere.

Two thousand women in a hotel conference lobby and nobody was gabbing? Mostly women were rooted to the carpet, not sure whether to go or to stay. If they had to talk, they whispered.

She and her cohorts fell equally silent as though their vocal cords had been vacuumed up like dust bunnies.

"Can you see what's going on?" she whispered to a tall woman standing near her.

"A rep was found dead in Longhorn C. Somebody said she'd been stabbed to death."

"Stabbed!" The word burst from her, and several people turned to stare. "At a Lady Bianca conference?" The last thing a convention based on positive thinking and beauty needed was some sordid murder in their midst.

"Any idea who the victim was?" she whispered to the same woman who'd given her the first information. She was over six feet tall and wore glasses so it was like standing beside the guy on a ship who is up in the crow's nest with the telescope.

She shook her head, but leaned down to murmur, "Lot of activity and cops hanging around."

Toni stepped forward, squeezing her way through the crush of well-dressed, well-coiffed, well-made-up women. As a fairly senior member of the organization she felt she might be needed. Besides, she was dying to see what was happening.

She '*scuse me'd* her way through the crush of women until she could see. The small conference room, Longhorn C, was where a dozen people could enjoy a breakout session or a meeting. Yellow crime scene tape stretched across the entranceway, but a further half circle of emptiness engulfed the doorway as though an invisible rope held everyone back. By craning her neck she could peek into the room. A flash went off as a guy with a camera took a picture of something on the floor. A technician was dusting the table for fingerprints. Another operated what looked like a black shop vac. His back was to her, and his jacket said Crime Scene Investigation.

While she stood there, a woman of about forty in a linen business suit, with her dark hair in a *take-me-seriously* chignon, emerged from the room. In a low voice, she gave her name to a uniformed officer standing near the door. All Toni could hear was "DA's office," and then she signed her name on a form held onto a metal clipboard, ducked under the tape and walked briskly toward the escalator. The Lady Bianca reps parted for her the way the Red Sea had parted for Moses.

Inside Longhorn C, a stretcher on wheels stood beside a clump of people in cop uniforms, plainclothes and one portly man with white hair in a black jacket that read *Coroner*. There was a shift of bodies and a sudden gap and she saw that they were sliding the victim into a body bag. She only saw the bottom part of the dead woman. Legs in Capri pants, open-toed sandals. Feet in crying need of a pedicure. As they maneuvered the body, a Birkenstock sandal fell off the woman's foot and a hand wearing a surgical glove picked it up and dropped it into the bag.

She watched a hand zip up the bag but couldn't hear it over the sound of the vacuum. They hoisted the body onto the gurney and then it rolled slowly out toward the hundreds of silent women, almost like a preview of the funeral procession. If Toni had been wearing a hat, she'd have removed it; as it was she tried to think of a suitable prayer or even a Bible verse as the body rolled by.

Two young uniformed cops—one male and one female—wheeled the gurney in her direction. Behind them walked the coroner wearing a suitably serious face. He sported a white mustache and the erect way he carried himself suggested to her that he'd once been in the military. Walking beside him, talking quietly was a guy in plain clothes who might as well have been in uniform. He had *cop* written all over him from his short haircut to his watchful eyes to his upright stance.

The black shape passed by where she stood and as she gazed toward it, she realized something obvious.

"That's not a Lady Bianca rep."

CHAPTER 2

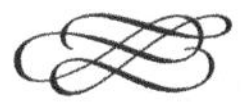

I have heard of your paintings too, well enough. God has given you one face, and you make yourselves another.

–William Shakespeare

Toni didn't realize she'd spoken aloud—and that she still had her volume turned high enough to pump up a thousand women—until the watchful eyes of the lone wolf cop zoomed in on her. He broke off his conversation with the coroner and addressed her directly.

"What did you say?"

"I said, 'That is not a Lady Bianca rep.'"

His expression didn't change and he didn't move quickly, but suddenly he was at her side. "Would you come with us, please, ma'am?"

Pleasant, but with the steel of command beneath. Exactly the tone she used at her weekly meetings with her sales associates.

"Of course, Detective."

He shot her a weird look like she might be psychic, but he looked exactly like the kind of actor who gets cast as a detective.

Mid-thirties at a guess. He had dark hair that wanted to curl, dark brown eyes, and a muscular build. Everything about him was emphatic. His eyes the color of good cocoa beans, the kind with a sheen. His hair was the same rich, dark brown and he had the muscular physique of a wrestler or a gym jock. He wasn't a whole lot taller than Toni in her heels. Five-eleven or so. But there was so much testosterone packed into that body she could feel it the way you can feel body heat coming off a person. The gurney bumped along and now she was following along too. It was becoming a parade.

She realized they were headed to the service elevator and wasn't given the option of not joining the ghoulish group.

The detective waited until the jaw-like gate creaked down on them, then asked, "Why did you say she's not with Lady Bianca?"

"Her shoes. The deceased woman is wearing Birkenstocks. Lady Bianca representatives wear closed-toed shoes at all times, along with skirts or dresses and hose. This woman is wearing sandals, no hose, cropped pants and her toenails aren't even polished. Definitely not Lady Bianca."

"Really," said the lone woman on the team.

Toni smiled at her. "We sell beauty products. It's important to look well-groomed and feminine while we do so." And, if anyone wanted Toni's opinion, that woman might find her work a little less grim if she wore a brighter shade of lipstick and made more of her big, dark eyes.

"And you are?"

"Toni Diamond. I'm a national sales director. I've been with the company for fifteen years, so I know pretty much everyone."

"And you can tell she's not in your organization by her shoes?" the detective asked.

"I only caught a glimpse of her legs. I don't have anything else to go on."

The detective hesitated. "Would you recognize her if you saw her face?"

Her gaze snapped to his. "I might."

The elevator creaked and cranked its way down. He glanced over at the coroner who shrugged and said, "Your call."

He reached over and unzipped the top part of the body bag. Toni moved closer to look, torn between fascination and horror. She tried to imagine this was a sleeping bag and the woman inside it was merely napping. But the face was too pale to keep up the fiction.

"Oh, poor thing. She's so young." The dead woman was in her early to mid-thirties with flyaway blonde hair. A pale blue T-shirt could be seen and the edges of a dark red bloodstain on the left side, above her heart.

Her left hand rested on her chest as though she'd reached for the wound as she died. Toni quickly moved her gaze to the woman's face and experienced a quick burst of relief on finding the woman was a stranger.

"I've never seen her before." But Toni was too honest, or maybe too outspoken, to leave it at that. "She's wearing Lady Bianca makeup, though. And it's a nice makeup job," Toni said, studying the face which would have been pretty in a nondescript way in life. In death, that makeup stood out like a mask.

"She didn't know enough to brace her elbows when she applied her lip liner." She glanced at the only other woman in the elevator who was still living. "That's why it's wavy around the edges."

"You can recognize Lady Bianca makeup?" the detective asked. His tone made it sound like a pretty unimpressive talent.

"I'm almost positive. The shadow trio on her eyelids is from our fall collection. Pumpkin spice, mulled cider, and hickory liner." She was genuinely puzzled. "Her make-up's Lady Bianca, but the rest of her doesn't match. Not the shoes. Not the T-shirt. Not the hands."

There were ink stains between the dead woman's thumb and forefinger, like she'd taken notes with a leaky pen.

"See how she hasn't taken care of her hands? The nails are bitten, no polish, and her skin is rough. This woman hasn't had a manicure in months. If ever." In comparison, Toni showed them her own hands, smooth of skin and shiny of nail. Her daughter might think that the tiny half moon of sparkles where the white part of her French manicure met the pink part was over the top, but then, at sixteen, Tiffany thought everything her mother did was over the top. Including breathing.

She wore a small collection of her prize rings, including the two-carat diamond she'd won when her sales team had the highest sales in the country three years ago. The dead woman wore a single silver ring with a Celtic design on it that badly needed cleaning.

"I've never known a sales rep who didn't come to the convention with a fresh manicure."

"But the woman *is* wearing Lady Bianca make-up," the cop reiterated.

Toni's brows pulled together in a frown that she automatically smoothed, determined to keep her face a Botox-free zone as long as possible. "I'm pretty sure she is, but other than that, she doesn't look like one of us."

The elevator bumped to a stop. "Thank you for your help." The detective pulled out a card and handed it to her. "If you think of anything that might be helpful, call me."

She read the name on the card aloud. "Detective Sergeant Luke Marciano. Major Crimes Unit."

Before they filled their hands with gurney, she pulled out a few of her own cards and handed each person one, starting with the woman who could certainly use Toni's help in the cosmetics department.

"Let me give you all my card. Give me a call and I'll be happy to give you or someone special in your life a complimentary makeover."

With varying expressions of disdain they all pocketed the card. Didn't matter. She was used to disdain and was philosophical about it. Of course, she'd never tried to market makeup over a corpse before, but she wasn't one to let any opportunity slip away.

She stayed inside the yawning cage of the elevator as the group wheeled the dead woman away, her gaze fixed on the female cop, already envisioning her in better makeup and hair.

The wheels of the gurney were bumping their way into the basement area of the hotel where the loading dock would be. As the group passed an industrial trash can the young male officer tossed her card in the garbage.

Okay. So no free makeover for his wife.

Even as the word makeover passed across her mind, the obvious truth hit her. Her gasp was louder than the creaking elevator. She dashed out after them, her heels clacking on the bare cement. "Wait. I figured it out. She must have had a makeover."

Her relief at finding out for sure that the dead woman wasn't a Lady Bianca rep was enormous. Not only did she not want to think of anyone in her business ending up...that way, but there was also a practical side to her relief. The convention could too easily be derailed by thousands of women gossiping about murder instead of learning about cosmetics.

The group moving the gurney stopped as one and turned to her.

"She's not a Lady Bianca associate at all," she announced. "I knew it the minute I saw those shoes. One of our representatives gave her a makeover, that's all."

"What makes you so sure?" asked Luke Marciano.

She pulled out another of her cards and waved it at them.

"Lady Bianca cosmetics are sold outside a retail environment. Offering makeovers is how we introduce ourselves and our products, like I just did to y'all. During the convention there are thousands of enthusiastic sales reps in and around the hotel. Someone offered this woman a makeover and she took them up on it. Which means she's not part of Lady Bianca. Obviously, you'll have to direct your efforts elsewhere."

Detective Marciano took a couple of steps toward her. "You're sure this woman couldn't possibly be connected to Lady Bianca?"

"I'd swear to it on my grandmother's grave. And I dearly loved my grandmother." Of course, Gran had been cremated so she didn't actually inhabit a grave. The urn containing her ashes occupied pride of place on the mantel of the electric fireplace her mama had bought at Walmart. They both looked real nice in the double-wide. Since, officially, there was no grave to swear on, Toni was more willing to take a flyer on the truth. But her gut told her this woman wasn't Lady Bianca and her instincts were rarely wrong.

The detective sent her a look that probably made murderers fall down on their quivering knees and confess.

"How many murders have you solved, Ms. Diamond?"

She smiled sweetly. "About as many as you've done makeovers." A muffled snort of amusement came from the other woman's direction.

Marciano seemed to be debating something. He stared at her and his right hand slipped into his pocket to jingle change. After a long moment, he said, "There were cosmetics found beside the body. Lady Bianca brand."

This didn't depress her. The news had the opposite effect. "A small package? With travel-sized samples in it?"

"Sounds about right."

She nodded, forcing herself to suppress her smile of relief out of respect for the recently departed. "It's the starter kit. We give it to all our makeovers. Encourages them to use the products, then they get hooked and become customers for life." She glanced at the black body bag, thinking the dead woman's life as a Lady Bianca customer had been extraordinarily short.

She wondered what that woman had done during her time on earth, and why she'd agreed to a makeover today of all days. Or maybe it had been yesterday.

He looked at the female cop. "If she's not a Lady Bianca rep, then who the hell is she?"

Toni figured it was a rhetorical question, but she answered him anyway. "I can't tell you that, but I can find out who gave her the makeover. We always get our clients' names and contact information when we do a makeover." She thought for a minute. "Can I see the makeup samples?"

Now the cop looked puzzled. "I thought you said giving out samples was standard procedure?"

"It is. But a good rep will customize the pack a little bit, choosing colors that will compliment a woman's coloring." She shrugged. "Some can't be bothered." She tried not to let the irritation she felt for such sloppy sales practices show in her tone, but if there was one thing she'd learned in more than fifteen years in the business, it was that attention to detail mattered. A woman whose Lady Bianca makeover left her looking fabulous was much more likely to spend her money on cosmetics than a woman who merely looked good.

"If I'd done that woman's makeup, I'd have gone with a softer palette. The pumpkin spice, mulled cider and hickory would look great on a brunette like you, ma'am, with your tawny skin tones and big brown eyes, but with this lady's white and pink tones and what I'm guessing are blue eyes, I'd have chosen our fall mauves and plum tones, I'd have feathered a little eggplant right—"

"Get to the point, ma'am. We're more interested in catching the killer than getting a lesson in cosmetics."

Well, he might be, but she could tell she'd caught the attention of the female cop.

"What that means is that whoever gave this poor woman her final makeover was either new, incompetent or had overbought on the tawny palette and was trying to push that stock."

The air down here smelled musty and under the harsh lighting the dust motes floating lazily in the air were the size of dandruff.

"The makeup package is upstairs. Find Detective Henderson and tell him Marciano sent you." He sent her a stern glance. "And you don't touch anything."

When she widened her eyes, her mascara-darkened lashes jabbed her as though she'd taken two forks to her eyelids. "Of course not. But it might give me a clue as to who did the makeover."

"If you find out who did it, you call me immediately. Don't approach the person yourself."

"But—"

"Ms. Diamond, this woman didn't die of old age."

CHAPTER 3

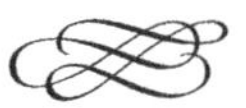

It is only shallow people who do not judge by appearances.

–Oscar Wilde

THE COPS WHEELED their gruesome cargo towards a loading dock with such casual assurance that a shiver crossed Toni's skin as she wondered how often in the past they'd had to perform the same task.

She turned away.

She'd never been in the service end of a hotel before. None of the fancy stuff here, she noted. The hotel behind the scenes was like a woman before she'd made herself up. Bare cement floors, industrial lighting, cinderblock walls—all of which had been covered over and prettied up out front for the public.

Not quite sure where she was, she decided to take the service elevator back the way she'd come.

When she'd taken those cards out to give them to the officers, she'd noticed a new text message on her phone. Her daughter, most likely.

Pulling her cell out of her bag, she saw she was right. The message read, *Nd mr Ilinr,* teen hieroglyphics for *Need more eyeliner*. No greeting or please or thank you or salutation. Extraordinary how a three-word message could drip with surliness. She didn't even have to specify color. Tiffany's current palette only contained one shade: black.

She took the service elevator up a floor and emerged into another cement floored hallway. A few steps led her into the kitchen. She must have got off the elevator a floor too soon, but, since she'd had enough of that cavernous metal cage, she kept going and got a sneak preview of the food for today's luncheon banquet.

White coated and capped kitchen help were busy at massive industrial ovens and the smells of baking bread and roasting meat would have made her mouth water under normal circumstances.

A female chef shouted orders to a harried looking underling and then glared at Toni as she edged through the organized bustle.

"Sorry," she whispered as she eased herself around a gleaming stainless prep counter where salads where being made in assembly line fashion. She headed for the nearest exit and found herself in the ballroom where lunch would be served. After the mayhem of the kitchen, the space looked huge and lonely with so many empty tables. A team of waiters were setting up, flipping lilac tablecloths onto the round tables.

Next door to the big ballroom was a conference room now set up as a Lady Bianca cosmetics store featuring everything from the full collection of products to the equally enormous array of prizes that could be won by hard-working sales associates.

Even in here she could tell that the atmosphere was

different than usual. Less upbeat, verging on somber. This would never do. The sooner they could prove that that poor dead woman was not associated with Lady Bianca, the quicker they could all get back to business.

After buying four of the thick kohl pencils Tiffany favored, and reminding herself once more that goth was a phase like any other, she checked her watch. Normally, she took a second to admire the way the twelve diamonds on its face twinkled, reminding her that every hour of her life was a sparkling opportunity. But now she noted that the next sessions had already started.

She hoped that with the body removed, the associates had gone ahead in and weren't gawping like buzzards fixin' to light into a dead possum.

She strode out into the corridor ready to play mother hen if she had to, and found Orin Shellenbach, VP of Sales for Lady Bianca, shepherding the last stragglers into sessions.

Once they'd all disappeared, she walked forward and poked her head inside Longhorn C.

"Crime scene, ma'am," a sharp voice greeted her. It belonged to a heavy-set black woman with a no-nonsense manner.

"I'm looking for Detective Henderson," she said.

The woman glared at her like she might be here to report a broken nail and they all had better things to do. "He's out interviewing."

"Any idea where?"

"Honey, I have enough trouble keeping track of my own people."

"Okay. Thanks for your help," she said, with all the sweetness in her, while taking a quick visual sweep of the area.

A man in blue overalls knelt on the ground and sliced the carpet around a dark, greasy looking bloodstain where the body had lain, and the fingerprint guy was spraying something on the walls. Otherwise, she was surprised how lacking in drama the scene looked. No broken glasses or overturned chairs. Apart from the bloodstain and the crime scene tape, the room looked ready to hold a meeting.

In the end, it didn't take enormous powers of sleuthing to find Detective Henderson. He'd set up in Longhorn B, where he was interviewing a cleaner. Henderson was in his fifties with iron-gray hair cut like a Marine's. A long, gaunt ribbon of a man, he had the lean and hungry look of someone who either runs marathons or has an eating disorder.

He scribbled in a notebook. She didn't want to interrupt, so she poured herself a glass of water from the ice water station in the corridor and stood sipping it. Not even in times of extreme stress did she neglect her eight glasses of water a day. She waited politely outside the open door, though the cleaner spoke clearly enough that she could hear every word.

The woman was Hispanic and her face was flushed either with anger or fear. Or maybe high blood pressure.

"You're absolutely sure there was no one in the conference room, Longhorn C," he glanced at his notes, "when you cleaned it at nine-twenty p.m. last night?"

"I already told you. There wasn't anybody."

"Did you see anyone in the area?"

"No. Nobody."

"Hear anything?"

She shook her head. "I had the vacuum going."

"Before you went into the room, where were you?"

"In this room. I do Longhorn A, then B, then C." Logical. Though Toni bet that if she had to clean hotels, she'd switch the order she cleaned rooms if only to make her routine a bit more interesting.

"And after you finished Longhorn C?"

The woman shrugged. "Then I went on my break. In the staff room downstairs."

"Did you come back up later?"

"No. I was finished in this part of the hotel. I did the bathrooms on the main floor after my break. Then I went home."

"Okay. Thank you for your help. If you remember anything, anything at all..."

"I got your card."

The woman walked off with a heavy tread, like she spent all day on her feet and they were getting tired of it. The detective glanced at his watch and then scribbled some more.

"Excuse me? Detective Henderson?"

He turned to her. His eyes were so undecided between gray and blue that they were virtually colorless. "Yes?"

"My name is Toni Diamond. I'm with Lady Bianca Cosmetics." She watched what little color was in his eyes leach out as though she not only didn't deserve his attention, but she didn't even deserve full ocular pigmentation.

"What can I do for you, ma'am?" Brisk. No time to waste.

"Detective Marciano asked me to have a look at the cosmetics you found on the...at the scene of the crime."

The blankness vanished. If anything, he now looked at her with suspicion.

If there was one thing she'd learned in her years of selling it was that with some people less is more in the talking department. Detective Henderson, she'd guess, was of the less is more school. She let him think about her request uninterrupted while he pinned her with that unnerving stare. Then he gave a sharp nod and said, "This way."

He led her back to Longhorn C and called over one of the technicians and asked for the makeup samples. They all wore coverings over their shoes so even Henderson wasn't going to go into that room without putting on special gear.

The technician was young enough that he still had a little acne on his forehead. "It's been bagged and tagged."

She got it. She wasn't going to open the big baggie thing and apply the eye makeup, even if there hadn't been a rusty red smudge in one corner of the Lady Bianca sampler pack that she didn't even want to think about.

He held it at eye level and she squinted at the starter kit. Henderson stood beside her so quiet and still she barely noticed him, but she felt his gaze on her face while she inspected the kit.

"That's odd," she said.

"What's odd?"

She turned sharply to find Detective Marciano at her elbow. She'd been so busy staring at the tiny case, trying to make sense of it that she hadn't heard him approach. Or maybe creeping was one of his detective talents.

"These samples?"

"Yeah," he sounded vaguely irritable. "Are they the same colors Jane Doe was wearing?"

"No. They aren't even this year's colors." She turned to him. "We haven't handed out those samples since last year."

Detectives Marciano and Henderson seemed a tad underwhelmed at the news that the woman had died with last year's sampler pack. Of course, to them it wouldn't mean anything.

"It's against the rules. Once the colors change, the sales rep is required to give out the new sampler packs."

They both nodded politely. "Thank you for your help, ma'am," Marciano said. This time he didn't even add the "if you think of anything call us," routine. Clearly, they didn't think she had much of value to offer the investigation.

If Toni were a believer in omens, she'd have to say that seeing a murder victim on the first morning of the annual conference wasn't a good one. She felt pretty shaken up by the experience, but she didn't have time to waste in self-indulgent moaning.

She needed to stop whoever was giving out old sampler packs

and the most efficient way she could think of to do that was to get hold of Orin Shellenbach and get him to send a reminder email to all the reps. Hopefully, he'd also find a way to reinforce the message to everyone who was right here at the conference.

She headed down the escalator to the main level and noticed that registration was still backed up. Lady Bianca associates had been registering for two days now and still the procession of women waiting to be checked in snaked like the world's slowest conga line.

No hotel they'd ever found could smoothly register several thousand women all arriving at once.

The reception desk, even fully staffed, couldn't hope to get through this many women in less than a couple of hours. But then the consultants were used to that. There they stood in long, curling lines. They'd come from every state in the union as well as Mexico and Canada. Some had flown and others had driven hours, even days to get here. And yet every one of them looked professionally turned out. Their hair was neat, their clothes businesslike. They wore hose and closed-toed shoes, various recognition pins and jewelry. And, of course, their makeup was flawless.

Even though they were standing with their luggage and the lines were barely inching forward, there was more excitement and happiness in this crowd than she'd seen—well, since last year's conference.

And the noise! The gals gossiped, giggled, traded war stories, introduced each other and inched toward the eight harried desk clerks.

Of course, no cohort of thousands is without its bad apples and as she hit the main level and stepped off the escalator, she saw one particularly moldy Golden Delicious coming toward her. The lobby was so crowded with women waiting to check in that only a narrow corridor was left to pass from one end to the other so it was impossible for her to avoid the only person in Lady Bianca she truly despised.

Nicole Freedman never met a corner she couldn't cut. If there was something she wanted, she'd lie, cheat and push out a few crocodile tears if necessary. Unfortunately, she and Toni were chief rivals for this year's top sales division prize. Not for the first time.

Toni donned a smile as fake as the diamonds on her suit buttons and said, "Well, hello, Nicole. You're looking wonderful." In fact, she'd gone a shade too dark in the hair dye on her sleek bob. With her pale complexion and the raven's wing hair, she reminded Toni of a much older version of Tiffany and her friends. Mom Goth—yeah, that was a trend that was going to be big.

As usual, Nicole was surrounded by a couple of groupies. Melody Feckler, her confidante, right hand and dog's body, had taken to dyeing her hair the same shade as her mentor, Toni noted. It wasn't much of a surprise since Melody tended to copy everything Nicole did. They wore similar suits and shoes, and carried the same bags, but it was clear that Nicole spent a lot more money on herself. Melody was like one of those magazine layouts where they show the designer runway model and then recreate the look with cheap imitations from lower end stores. Melody had a sweet face and candid blue eyes, but with the black hair she looked like Snow White's older, overweight cousin.

Stacy Krump was a newer recruit. An intense, quiet woman who looked like the type of girl in high school who cried if she didn't get an A. From the number of recognition pins on her chest, she was still getting straight A's.

Nicole registered almost as much phony delight at seeing Toni as she'd been accorded.

"Why, honey, you look better every time I see you. And you

are obviously using the new highlighter shades to minimize your nose. Really, in this light, it hardly looks prominent at all."

Every woman has her vulnerable spot. Her thighs are too big, her breasts too small, her teeth too crooked. Toni's thing was her nose. She had a big nose. Not Cyrano de Bergerac get-a-nose-job-and-get-on-with-your-life big, but her nose was the dominant feature on Toni's face.

She'd inherited it from her father and on a six-foot-two rodeo rider it looked fine. On Toni it looked like there'd been a bit of a glitch on the genetic assembly line. Her grandmother, the Pentecostal preacher's wife, who'd never been known for diplomacy or keeping her thoughts to herself, used to say that it was God's punishment to Toni for being so nosy.

Of course, Toni grew into her nose as she grew older and she'd learned how to play up her good features, her eyes and mouth, so she'd didn't worry about it much anymore, but back in the early days when they'd been friends, she'd foolishly confided in Nicole about her Achilles nose.

There were a lot of rejoinders Toni could make, most of which included the term undead, but she tried to model good behavior, especially in front of sales associates, so she let the jibe pass, merely saying, "The colors this season are fantastic."

She turned to Melody Feckler. "Can you believe that line? I hope you checked in early."

"The great thing is we've been here a couple days already. Nicole wanted us to have some team bonding time. How about you?"

"I checked in yesterday morning. I always come early to get myself organized and avoid this," she gestured to the barely moving crowd. "It will be midnight before everybody gets their room. Are you and Stacy rooming together this year?"

Most attendees bunked in with one to three roommates to share costs. Nicole never shared a room at the conference. Toni didn't either now she could afford to have her privacy, but most of the sales reps shared.

Melody shook her head looking awfully pleased with herself. "My husband works for this hotel chain back home in Oklahoma City. He's on the front desk." She leaned closer and whispered, "I'm not supposed to spread it around, but he was able to get me a room here for next to nothing. It means I don't have to have a roommate." She leaned even closer. "He might even come visit me. With both of us working so hard, we almost never get any time away at a hotel."

"That's great," she said warmly. "Of course I'll keep it to myself."

"Looks like we're in fierce competition again for the top sales division prize," Nicole reminded her, as though she could possibly have forgotten.

"That's right. It's so exciting that the final orders don't close until the end of the month. Right in the middle of the conference. Should be a nail-biter."

Or, in Nicole's case, a backstabber.

CHAPTER 4

Look your best—who said love is blind?

–Mae West

NATURALLY, the talk at lunch was all about the murder. The poor luncheon speaker was going to have to give the equivalent of the Gettysburg Address to get any attention.

Toni and her top salespeople had met in advance so they could sit together and as the doors opened and the women filed in for lunch, they reached a table that still had plenty of seats at the same moment that Melody Feckler cried, "Here's three together."

Nicole and Toni gave each other another fake smile and made the most of sharing the table. If you didn't grab groups of seats when you saw them, another team would scoop them from under you. Rather like musical chairs without the music.

Toni ended up sitting beside Stacy Krump, who flanked

Nicole's right while Melody sat to her left. Beside Toni was Ruth Collier, a retired schoolteacher who ran her skincare classes as though there'd be a test at the end, but had a true gift for sales, and Suzanne Mireille, a half-Cuban half-French-Canadian woman whose café con leche-colored skin was a glowing billboard for Lady Bianca's Luminescence line. She'd come to Dallas with her pilot husband and was busy raising three boys and a girl while selling makeup on a part-time basis. Her native tongue was French, but she was equally comfortable in English or Spanish, a definite asset.

Four other women completed the table: Donna Ray Atkins, whose family owned a pig farm in Kansas, and three others from her region.

As the scant details of the morning's death were being chewed over as thoroughly as the salads Toni had seen in the kitchen, Melody Feckler leaned forward and said, "I heard that there was blood everywhere."

"There would be," Donna Ray agreed, nodding. She had the breadbasket in her hand and was in the act of choosing between the seeded whole wheat rolls and the small white crusty ones. "It's the same when we gut the pigs on the farm. We stick 'em right over a drain and the blood still gets all over us, the walls, the floor...blood everywhere." She held the basket aloft. "Would anyone like a bread roll?"

No one did, so she put the basket down and proceeded to split and butter the white roll. "A grown woman or man would have about as much blood to spill, I expect. Was an artery cut, do you know? 'Cause that'll really cause the blood to spurt. I'm not kidding. It's like you turned on the garden hose and then put your thumb over the end." She demonstrated and made a noise that Toni assumed was an approximation of the sound of water spraying from a hose. Or blood from an open artery.

"When we slaughter our pigs, we hit the carotid artery and the jugular." She mimed slashing her own throat. "You'd be amazed how fast the animal drains. Most of it's out in five minutes." She nodded, looking around at them all. "That's how I'd kill someone. Slash their throat. If you do it from behind, you could be quick and if you cut through the trachea, they'd die without making a sound."

Toni watched the woman's muscular arms as she gestured. "You think the killer could be a woman?"

Donna Ray looked at her and gave her a slow smile. "If I wanted you dead, Toni, you wouldn't stand a chance." It wasn't a boast. "Somebody reasonably fit and determined? Sure."

"What if the throat wasn't slashed? What if they were stabbed in the front?"

"Ribs are your biggest issue. Get through them, hit the heart, and the deed's done."

The salads were removed and the wait staff began placing plates in front of everyone. "Oh, good," Toni said to Ruth, looking down at the pale rounds of meat on her plate, "roast pork."

As a dieting technique, Toni decided that discussing a brutal murder with a woman who butchered animals on a regular basis was extremely effective. She wasn't the only one who pushed the meat around her plate.

Orin Shellenbach rose while they were eating and began congratulating everyone on making the commitment to themselves and their businesses and coming to the convention. Because the room was so large, they'd rigged up a projection screen behind him so he loomed over them all in close up. Toni watched the flash of white teeth in his tanned face. The man spent so much time on a tanning bed, he was starting to look radioactive. He was their usual MC since he combined the flashy good looks of a game show host with the natural charm of a snake oil salesman.

"After you finish that delicious lunch, we've got a world-renowned expert in sales techniques, Lara Lester, to speak to us on *Five Ways to Turn No into Yes*."

"I wish I knew five ways to turn this pork into tofu," Ruth whispered in Toni's ear.

"I'm just glad my daughter, the vegan PETA crusader, isn't here."

"There's a rumor the dead woman was a new Lady Bianca rep," Ruth continued in the same low voice.

"I'm sure she wasn't," Toni said and related her own part in the affair.

"Oh, my God. You mean he unzipped the...thingy and you saw her?"

"Yeah." She pushed her plate away.

"And you're sure she couldn't be Lady Bianca?"

"Look around you. Who in this room is wearing cropped pants and sandals? I even went and looked at the check-in line at registration. Everyone was dressed properly."

"How weird that she'd have one of our makeovers right before she died."

"I know. I really wish she'd gone to the hotel salon. The police are convinced we have something to do with the death."

When dessert arrived—the normal signal that the keynote speaker was about to begin—Orin took the microphone once more and asked for everyone's attention. As Toni looked to the front of the room and the stage area she noticed the two detectives from earlier, Marciano and Henderson, standing to the side of the podium. What on earth?

"As I'm sure you all know, there was a very unfortunate incident this morning where a woman died," Orin said. Toni almost smiled. Trust Orin, the master spin doctor, to refer to a brutal murder as an unfortunate incident.

"The police will be circulating among you with some photographs of the recently departed. I know that we will all give the police our full cooperation. If you recognize this woman or have any information at all, please give it to the police officers. The sooner we get this unpleasantness over with, the sooner we can go back to an inspiring and exciting conference, and *Five Ways to Turn No into Yes.*"

"Amen to that," Toni said.

Of course, it was impossible to relax with cops, both uniformed and plainclothes, going from table to table and circulating pictures of the dead woman.

Toni took a bite of her dessert, which was some kind of cheesecake with an unfortunately bright red sauce dripping over it like...well, she just couldn't summon the enthusiasm. She put her fork back down.

The women at her table managed to keep small talk going but it was obvious they were all on edge waiting for their turn with the photos.

It was a young guy in uniform who got to them, handing Donna Ray the photograph first. "I'd like each of you to look carefully at this picture and let me know if you've ever seen the lady before," he instructed. The picture that was passed around the table was a standard 8 x 10 glossy. Cropped high enough to miss the bloodstains on the woman's shirt, while still showing as much of the blue T-shirt as possible, so if you looked quickly it could look as though the woman was sleeping. On a metal table. And she was very pale.

Some of the women looked at the picture for a long time—the way people driving by a traffic accident stop and stare—and a couple of the women glanced as briefly as possible and then passed the photo along with a negative shake of the head.

Nicole Freedman took a cursory glance and passed the photo on as though touching it were beneath her notice. "Too negative. Stacy, don't spend any more time than you have to looking at it."

But Stacy's gaze was already glued to the photograph and she'd gone almost as pale as the woman in the picture. She glanced at Nicole first, nervously, then licked her lips and said in a half whisper, "I gave this woman a makeover yesterday."

"What?"

She pushed the photograph back toward Nicole. "Remember? We did the makeover in your room. I guess I recognize her because I spent so much time on her face."

"That can't be the same girl."

"It is."

"You're sure, ma'am?" the young officer asked her. He'd perked right up now that he had some action.

She stared at the photograph another moment, flicked another glance at Nicole, and then nodded. "Yes. I'm sure."

He signaled to Detective Marciano, who must have been on the lookout for a positive ID. He strode immediately to their table. He took in all the women at a glance. His gaze rested briefly on Toni and then kept going.

"This woman here says she gave Jane Doe a makeover," the uniformed officer said, indicating Stacy, who looked confused at his words.

"Her name wasn't Jane."

Marciano shot a frustrated glance at the uniformed officer, then a much kinder one at Stacy. "Do you know what her name was?"

"Violet."

"Violet?"

"Yes. I remember because I thought it was so pretty. Like a flower."

Marciano had his notebook out. "What time did you give Violet the makeover?"

Melody glanced at Nicole. "Around four?"

Her team leader nodded. "Sounds right. I can check in my book, Detective, to give you the exact time."

"You were both there?"

"That's correct."

Toni hadn't had a chance to talk to Orin yet about those outdated sampler packs and now it seemed as though she wouldn't have to. Nicole and Stacy were responsible. She could hardly believe it.

"Okay. Do you mind if we go back to wherever you gave that makeover? I'd like to take you back through the whole process and sometimes it's easier to remember details if you return to the scene."

"Is that okay, Nicole? It's your room and all."

Nicole jerked to her feet. "Yes, of course. But for heaven's sake, let's get going and get this over with."

"Fine by me," said Marciano.

"Is it okay if I tag along?" Toni asked Stacy, knowing she was only slightly less intimidated by Toni than she was by Nicole.

"Well, I guess. I mean, it's Nicole's decision but I—"

"I think it helps to have familiar faces around when you go through a stressful event, don't you?"

"Um, yeah. I guess so."

What Toni really wanted to find out was which of them was palming off last year's sampler packs on makeover candidates.

Nicole didn't realize Toni had tagged along until she entered the hotel room right behind Stacy.

"What are you doing here?" she demanded.

"I think Stacy wanted the extra support."

Nicole might have argued but by this time Marciano was in the room and he'd shut the door behind them. Throwing Toni out was only going to make Nicole look bad, so she contented herself with a glare and sat down in the chair behind the room's desk. Stacy, always one to follow the leader, took the other armchair.

That left Toni with the bed. She perched on the end, as far as she could get from where Nicole laid her head and hatched her evil plans.

Marciano pulled out his notebook and remained standing.

"You said her name was Violet?"

"Violet Hunter, Detective."

"Violet Hunter. You're sure?"

"Violet's card is right here." Nicole removed one of the customer information cards from her desktop. "We always have our makeover customers fill out a card so we can contact them later. This should give you everything you need." Her tone held an implied parenthetical (and stop interrupting the Lady Bianca conference). For once in her life, Toni was in full agreement with Nicole.

She handed him the card. "Here's your victim, Detective."

CHAPTER 5

A woman without makeup is like a rose without petals.

–Lady Bianca

THE INFORMATION CARD was about as useful as Luke had expected it to be. On a scale of one to ten, this information was a solid zero.

He glanced up from the card, a pre-printed affair emblazoned with the Lady Bianca logo, a stylized L and B entwined together with a crown sitting atop. The card stock was the same color as the tablecloths and balloons in the ballroom and most of the packaging for the Lady Bianca cosmetics. A putrid shade of pale purple.

Nicole Freedman looked down her nose at him as though she'd solved his case for him. Now she had places to be, and he was wasting her time. Stacy Krump was pleating her skirt with nervous fingers and gazing at him as though hoping for praise.

The only one not looking his way was Toni Diamond. Her gaze was on Nicole and she seemed troubled by something.

He spoke to Stacy. "The address she gave is in Washington State. How useful could that be if your business is in Texas?"

Nicole answered, "In fact, we're from Oklahoma, but Stacy would contact the rep who lives closest to the customer and she would get a referral fee, a small percentage of all that customer's future purchases. The program's very successful."

What wasn't "very successful" in the Lady Bianca world?

"Violet Hunter," he read aloud. "221B Baker Street, Seattle, Washington." He glanced up. "I'm guessing none of you ladies is a Sherlock Holmes fan?"

Stacy and Nicole Freedman shook their heads. Toni jerked her head as her attention switched from Nicole to him. She mouthed a soundless "O".

"Yes, 221B Baker Street is the fictitious address in London where Sherlock Holmes lived. Violet Hunter was a character. *The Copper Beeches*, I think."

"Copper..." Stacy looked confused.

"One of the Holmes stories."

"You mean Violet gave me a fake address?" She flipped her long blonde hair over her shoulder and stared at him through sad eyes. He wondered whether she was more disappointed about being lied to or about losing her referral income.

"Yep." He flicked the card between his fingers. "And I doubt her name's Violet."

"It happens," Toni said. "Sometimes they don't want to be contacted. Maybe they only want the free makeover, and of course don't like to admit that so they give us false data. But why choose Washington? It's possible she lived there."

"Or she figured even...you people would clue in to the fact that she wasn't from London, England, so she picked a state far away from where she truly lives." He focused on Stacy. "Did you two talk at all during the makeover?"

"Of course. A little. Mostly I explained all the products to her and showed her how to apply them. It's what we're supposed to do," she said, shooting a half-scared glance at the dark-haired woman at her side.

"What time did you finish the makeover?"

"It takes about an hour. So around five."

"Why did she want one?"

The women all looked at each other as if to say, "Only a man would ask why a woman might want a makeover."

"She had a date last night."

"A date? You're sure?"

"That's what she said."

"She definitely said 'date'—not 'appointment' or 'meeting'?"

Stacy closed her eyes for a moment and he waited. She opened her eyes. "I'm pretty sure it was a date. We talked about earrings."

"Earrings. Great. Did she mention the name of this guy she was dating?"

"She didn't say, sorry."

"What time they were getting together?"

Stacy shook her head.

"Was she staying at the hotel?"

"I didn't ask. She didn't have a suitcase or anything with her. But she was standing in the lobby when I went up to her, so maybe."

"Did she happen to mention where she was going on this date? Anything at all?"

She bit her lip, thinking hard, but shook her head again.

"How did you meet this woman? You said she was in the lobby?"

"Right. I walked up to her and complimented her on her pretty blue eyes. It's what we're supposed to do. Compliment women on their features and start up a conversation. It's called 'friendly fishing.'"

He wished quite suddenly that he had a female partner who could help him out here. Henderson would be as lost as he was. "Friendly fishing?"

"That's right. If you admire a woman's hairstyle, then why not go right up to her and say so? It's a great way to get into a conversation, plus you've made someone feel better about themselves." She beamed. "Then we offer the makeover."

"Anything at all you can remember about her would be helpful."

"Well, there was one thing."

He raised his notebook. "What?"

"Her skin was very dry. It sucked up the moisturizer like there was no tomorrow."

Well, that should wrap things up. "Mind if I take the card with me?"

"Of course not."

Toni looked up at him from her perch on the bed. "We know one other thing about that woman."

"What?"

"She knew her Sherlock Holmes."

TONI DEBATED RAISING the issue of the sampler pack, but she decided to wait until Marciano was gone. Giving out expired sampler packs wasn't a murder issue, it was a Lady Bianca matter. So, when he did his usual spiel about calling him if they thought of anything else, he left them and she stayed put.

Nicole looked at Toni pointedly when she didn't rush to leave. Toni didn't want to spend an extra second in Nicole's company any more than Nicole wanted her there, but she needed to find a subtle way to accuse the woman of breaking company rules.

"Well," Nicole said, "we've all got things to do."

"Right." She didn't move from the bed. "Stacy, I'm wondering, which sampler pack did you give the woman we're calling Violet?"

There was a moment of deathly silence. Stacy fidgeted and looked at Nicole. *Aha, gotcha.*

"I have some in my room, but..." Stacy began then glanced at Nicole again, who picked up the story.

"Stacy has a roommate so we thought it would be better to do the makeover here. Unfortunately, I didn't bring any sampler packs. But then I don't normally do makeovers during convention week."

"So, you're saying you sent your makeover off without a sampler pack?" *Liar.*

Nicole's eyes hardened and held Toni's gaze in a challenge. "Yes. Just as well as it happens. If the woman gave a fake name, she was hardly interested in becoming a lifelong customer. She only wanted a free makeover."

"Well," Toni said brightly to Stacy, "if you do any more makeovers, come and see me. I've got lots of sampler packs."

"Oh, so have I," Stacy jumped in, "in my room, but Violet—the woman—didn't want to wait. She was in a hurry for her date. So I said I'd get her one when I saw her."

"And did you?"

"No. I never saw her again."

Toni stood and brushed the back of her skirt, like a kid getting rid of Nicole cooties. "I guess I'd better go." Before she said something she'd regret. Bad enough that Nicole was lying to her face, but having Stacy expand on the lie only made it worse.

CHAPTER 6

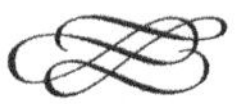

My face looks like a wedding cake left out in the rain.

–W.H. Auden

TONI WAS on her way back to her room to freshen up before the afternoon sessions started when her cell phone buzzed. Her mom.

"Hi Mama, what's up?"

"Oh, honey, I'm all in a panic." The familiar tone of her mother's voice had a second's dread stabbing her in the chest.

"Mama? Is Tiffany okay?"

"She's fine. She wants to talk to you in a minute, but I needed to speak to you first."

"What is it?" Her heartbeat slipped back to normal. If Tiffany was okay, the panic was going to be one of the mini soap operas that made up Linda Plotnik's life. Other people lived life by days. Linda lived hers in episodes with enough high dramatic peaks that you could schedule commercial breaks.

"I'm not calling you as my daughter, but as my boss," she warned.

"Okay. I'm ready." One of her big thrills had been recruiting her own mother as a Lady Bianca rep. And Linda was surprisingly good. She lived in the most glamorously populated mobile home park in all of Texas, Toni bet. Now, if Toni could only get her daughter interested in selling Lady Bianca to the teenaged crowd, they'd have a three-generation direct selling powerhouse.

"I did the craziest thing," Linda said in the Georgia accent that hadn't softened in a quarter century of living in Texas. "I invited my singing group to a makeup party at my place, only when I checked my beauty supplies, I discovered I was short a ton of stuff."

This was not the first time Toni had received one of these calls.

"Mama, you have to think these things through. You have to put in your order at the end of the month—you know that. I can put in an order for you today that will hit the cutoff for this month, but the stock won't be here for a couple of weeks. Don't plan a big party if you're low on stock."

"Oh, honey, I always think about the party first and then check my supplies. I know it doesn't work that way, but sometimes I forget. Could I get you to bring me over some things and we'll sort it out when you do your next order?"

"I'm at the convention, Mama, I can't—"

"Tiffany's helping me and we're really excited about the makeup party."

"Tiff's going to help?" Usually she couldn't get her daughter within a hundred miles of a Lady Bianca event. Except the one time she and her friends had picketed the home party Toni was appearing at—carrying PETA signs and shouting, "End Animal Cruelty." Lady Bianca didn't even use animal-tested products.

Of course, she should say no. But then her mom would have to cancel her party, and Tiffany wouldn't have a chance to help out. Besides, there was a reason her mom made such a great rep. She could sell. "This is the last time, Mama."

"I knew I could count on you, honey. I'll email you the list right away."

"When's the party?"

There was a tiny silence. She could hear a whisper and a giggle that had to be her daughter in the background. "Tomorrow night."

The store here was mostly for new products, with a few of the basics, but they wouldn't have everything Linda needed. Which meant she was going to have to drive all the way home to her place, an hour in one direction, take the stock from her own supplies, drive back in time for tonight's banquet dinner, and then get up early and drive everything another hour in the opposite direction to her mother's. Which meant missing at least two sessions tomorrow.

She could be a cutthroat businesswoman when she had to be, but when her mom and her daughter tag-teamed her, she was putty in their hands. She knew it, they knew it.

"Keep the coffee pot on, Mom. I'll see you in the morning."

"Thanks, hon. I knew I could count on you."

She was still reminding herself she had to get tougher with her mother, when she walked through the lobby, heading for the car park, and all but smacked into Nicole Freedman and Melody Feckler. Another crime to place at her mother's door. If she hadn't been rehearsing the tough love speech she was going to give her mom in the morning, she'd have seen the pair in plenty of time to avoid them.

"Hey, Toni, did you hear the latest?" Melody said, thereby

making it impossible for her to smile and keep going. *Oh, dear God, let there not be any more death and drama.*

"What is it?"

"The new diamond hard eyebrow pencil. They're ahead of schedule in production. We should have full stock before the fall."

Instinctively, she looked to Nicole for confirmation. The woman nodded. "It's true. Orin told us. Of course, it's not for everybody to know," she said, frowning at Melody. "He'll announce it tomorrow."

"That's wonderful. I think it's going to be a big seller." And might just get everybody back on track for the conference.

"Oh, I know it is."

Toni made a move to leave but Melody made a choking sound and her mouth flew open.

"Melody? Are you all right?"

"Thomas!" she cried, her face lighting up.

"Thomas? Who's Thomas?"

"My husband. I can't believe he's here. No, don't go, Toni. I want you to meet him."

Nicole did not look overjoyed. Husbands never came to these things. It wasn't outlawed or anything, but a sort of unwritten rule applied. No spouses or kids at the convention. Too distracting.

Apparently, Melody didn't get the memo, for her plump face was one big smile now she'd overcome the shock of seeing him.

Curious, because she was always curious to see who was paired with whom in love and life, she followed Melody's gaze.

Thomas Feckler was...crisp. It was the first adjective that popped to mind. His hair was perfectly cut, his casual clothes so well-pressed they gave the same impression of formality as a three-piece suit. He was clean shaven with a pleasant face that was neither handsome nor homely, but somewhere in-between.

His lips curved when he spotted his wife and his pace quickened to reach her.

"I'm so happy to see you," she said and threw her arms around him.

He squeezed her in a warm hug, then held her away from him, gazing into her face with concern. "I came the second I heard about the murder. Are you all right?"

Okay, so all the news crews and reporters cruising the lobby hadn't been here to cover the Lady Bianca convention opening, but the murder was a bigger story than she'd realized if the buzz had gone out of state.

"Of course, I am. I'm fine. But it's just awful. That poor woman."

"I'm so sorry. Shh. Try not to think about it."

"No. You're right. I'm so glad you're here." She pulled back. "Oh, and where are my manners? Thomas, this is Toni Diamond. She's one of our national directors."

"Ms. Diamond." His handshake was perfect. Firm, but not "Look how much testosterone I can pump" firm. And he took care of his hands, she was happy to note.

"And this is Nicole Freedman." She giggled. "I can't believe you've never met each other before. I know I talk about you to each other all the time."

"I'm so delighted to meet you at last," Nicole gushed, raising a hand so covered in diamonds her glitter rivaled that of the massive chandelier above them. If she won another division sales championship she was going to have to start sticking the rings on her feet. Or her horns.

"My pleasure," he said, taking her hand.

Then he turned back to Melody. "I've come to take you home."

"Home?" the three of them echoed in unison.

He glanced from one to the other. "Of course. You should all go home. They're saying a Lady Bianca rep was murdered. Have they caught the killer?"

"No," Toni said. "But they only found the dead woman this morning."

"It could be some psycho killing off sales reps. For all you know any one of you could be next. I checked with the front desk and already they've had cancellations and women heading home early."

"But we can't leave," Melody said. "Besides, Toni says it's not a Lady Bianca rep at all. It's terrible, of course, tragic, but we have to go on."

"Melody, please."

Nicole took his arm. "I'm telling you, Thomas, your wife is really going places. She needs to be here." She lowered her voice and leaned closer to him. "I can always tell the ones who have the passion and talent to go all the way in this company. Melody is a true star. She'll be parking her dream car in the garage of your new mansion in no time."

Toni knew the patter. In truth, she'd used the same lines herself when she'd been excited about a star recruit. But she didn't feel like staying to hear Nicole's sales job.

Melody placed her plump hands on her husband's chest. "Honey, I can't go home. This conference means everything to me."

Toni was about to excuse herself and slide out of the conflict zone when she witnessed a remarkable thing. Thomas Feckler leaned his forehead against his wife's and said, "Well, if you're not leaving, then I guess I'm staying."

"You're serious?"

"Somebody's got to watch your back."

She said her goodbyes, promised Melody's husband she'd be careful, and wondered what her life would have been like if Duane had turned out to be the kind of guy who stuck by his wife when times were tough instead of lighting out for parts unknown the second there was trouble.

She guessed she'd never know.

CHAPTER 7

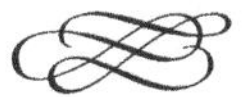

I'm not offended by all the dumb blonde jokes because I know I'm not dumb...and I also know that I'm not blonde.

–Dolly Parton

LUKE HAD BARELY ENTERED the hotel the next morning when he saw Toni Diamond heading toward the car park elevator. If possible, her hair seemed even bigger than it had the day before. And blonder. She was fully decked out in another one of those power suits, this one a soft green, and high heels that sparkled when the light hit whatever fake baubles were splashed over the front.

"Ms. Diamond?" he called out.

She turned. "Mornin', Detective. I'm in kind of a hurry."

He caught up with her. "I have some questions about how your company works." And there was something about her that told him he could trust her. Her eyes were such an amazing color between blue and green that he suspected fake lenses, to match everything else that was fake, from her hair color to her nails. But there was a gleam of intelligence behind those eyes, and she'd been right about that makeover.

She lasered him with her gaze. "Detective, I don't want to tell you your business, but there is no way that woman's death is connected with Lady Bianca."

"She had a makeover and then she died."

"If she had died after eating in a restaurant, would you interrogate the owners on how they ran their operation?"

"If we had reason to believe there was a connection, yes."

She pushed the elevator button with the flat of her finger, careful not to muss her fake nail. She was a tall woman in her heels. Only a couple of inches shorter than him. "How can there be a connection? You don't even know who she was. That woman's purse was missing. Surely the thief murdered her?"

"Maybe. But she was found with samples of your makeup, and you figured she was wearing Lady Bianca stuff. It's about the only thing we know about her."

"And that she read mysteries and was left-handed."

He shot her a glance.

"There were ink stains between the thumb and forefinger of her left hand."

He nodded. Okay, he was impressed. He'd figured she was smarter than she looked, but in fact, she was a lot smarter than she looked. So he leveled with her. "Maybe there's no connection, but maybe there is. Maybe she was going to change into her fancy suit and closed-toed hose and pin on her name badge, so covered with jewels you couldn't read her name, anyway. But she never got the chance."

"But—"

"And she died on the convention level, which has been

taken over by the Lady Bianca conference, in a meeting room reserved by Lady Bianca."

"But—"

"I'll only take a half hour of your time."

She smiled, her perfect pink lips curving in a perfect pink crescent. "You'll need a couple of hours."

He held his expression to neutral. "I'm not planning to sign up as a rep, Ms. Diamond."

She waved a hand in the air and there were so many rings on it he was surprised she could lift her wrist. "I've got to deliver some product to my mother this morning. She's one of my reps. If you want to come along with me, I can tell you all about Lady Bianca while we drive. That's why it will take a couple of hours. Otherwise you'll have to wait until I get back."

He debated for a few seconds, but Henderson had the hotel under control and his gut told him that Lady Bianca was the key to all of this. Besides, Toni Diamond might look like the Queen of the Airheads, but she'd proved to be both observant and smart. So, he said, "Fine," and followed her into the elevator.

Her car was a surprise. He'd expected something big and flashy that would guzzle so much fuel it needed its own oil well, but in fact, she drove a hybrid. A putrid color that reminded him of Easter baskets.

"Interesting car color," he said when he got in.

She beamed at him. "It's lilac, the Lady Bianca signature color."

"Naturally."

At least she drove well, Luke thought, as they made their way through intermittently heavy traffic in her rolling Easter egg, navigating through town and then heading south on 35E.

"All right, Detective. You've got me all to yourself for two hours. What do you want to know?"

"You sound like a Columbo re-run."

She laughed. "Except that you don't wear a bad raincoat and I'm not a suspect." She glanced at him. "Am I?"

"No. And you can call me Luke."

Her glance was like a splash of the Caribbean. Who would buy lenses that fake? "That definitely makes me not feel like a suspect. I can't imagine you telling America's Most Wanted to call you Luke."

"No."

"Then I guess you'd better call me Toni."

"You're a good driver, Toni."

"Thanks."

He shifted so he could see her better. "I need to know how Lady Bianca works." He didn't tell her that he'd whiled away a couple of hours last night reading websites devoted to trashing Lady B. Seemed not everybody loved the company as much as Toni Diamond.

"No leads yet?"

"We're working on several angles." He said, giving his standard response to civilian inquiries. But so far there wasn't much to go on. Nobody who should have checked out of the hotel and didn't, or should have checked in and didn't. No missing person report filed and Jane Doe had never been fingerprinted.

"Well, since you're giving me your company on a long drive, I'll tell you what I can. Lady Bianca's not complicated. We sell the best cosmetics in America, we're all independent businesswomen—and a handful of men—and we market our products through home parties, by giving makeovers and through word of mouth." Even though she sounded like a talking sales brochure, there was something almost naïve about her enthusiasm.

"Why would someone buy your makeup and not just go to the mall for whatever they need?"

"You can't buy Lady Bianca through a mall. It's only available through your independent representative. That means you get personal service. I know my clients. I know the colors and products they like and I keep a record of everything. You may not realize your foundation is running out, but if you haven't reordered in three months, you'll get a call from me. Even if you still have plenty left, you should always replace foundation after three months," she told him. "Otherwise it can harbor bacteria."

"I'll be sure and remember that."

Her lips, glossy as a centerfold's, tilted in a smile. "I'm a woman's personal beauty consultant. I stay on top of trends and new makeup techniques, I always know the latest colors and I help women make the most of themselves. I will personally deliver product to a woman's home, help her host her own party and, if she's interested and has the right attitude, I'll help her start her own business."

"Is there much money in Lady Bianca?"

"As much as you're willing to work for. When I first started, I was a real sob story. A single mom with nothing. Today, my clothes aren't held together with safety pins, but with diamond buttons." Fake diamonds but he understood what she was getting at. "I make good money, drive a pretty purple car and live in a beautiful home I paid for myself thanks to Lady Bianca."

"Do most women do as well as you?"

"No. Some are in it for part-time extra income, some really only want to get the product at wholesale and some are working harder than I do and making a whole lot more money. Our company is based purely on selling a great product through hard work and talent." She glanced at him. "Now I've answered your questions. How about you answer a couple for me?"

He shifted on the seat. "What kind of questions?"

"What can you tell me about the murder?"

"Not much."

She tapped a glittery thumb against the steering wheel. "I guess I feel a little bit connected because of yesterday morning. I can keep my mouth shut, you know."

"I can tell you that she was stabbed to death."

"I could see that for myself. She was attacked from the front." Toni mimed a stabbing motion toward her own chest. "Did she know her killer?"

"Possibly. No sign of struggle and no defensive wounds. But the killer could have got her before she had a chance to react. It's a hotel. You don't automatically distrust a stranger coming up to you."

"Nobody heard her scream?"

"No. But it's pretty quiet on the convention floor at night. If she'd cried out, who'd have heard her?"

"So she was killed at night?"

"Educated guess puts death around eleven."

She tapped her thumb against the steering wheel again. "You think it's an isolated incident?"

"What we're trying to do is put together the story of her life, especially her recent life. Somewhere, somehow she angered someone badly enough to kill her."

"But her life's not in Corvallis. All we know is that she was at the hotel. We don't even know if it was for a few hours or a few days."

"Well, if her life's not here, something—or someone—out of it followed her."

"You're certain it couldn't be a random act of violence?"

He shook his head. "Could be but I don't think so."

"Her purse was missing. Couldn't the motive be robbery?"

"Depends what was in her purse. If it was a few bucks and some credit cards, it wasn't worth killing for. If it's more, then how did the killer know? We're back to her past following her here."

He shifted so he could search her face. He always felt some

personal connection with the victims, more as he got to know of them and their lives. He understood that Toni felt some connection too. Whatever evidence of sleeplessness might be there she'd covered up. "Did you get any sleep last night?"

She made a wry face. "Not much. I kept seeing her."

"It's never easy." He didn't bother telling her that insomnia was one of his hobbies. "But don't worry. Chances are the killer's long gone. And hopefully left enough evidence behind that we can get him or her off the streets."

Up ahead was a sign that read Pecan Villa Estates. She put her right turn signal on, then she swung the car through a gap in the manicured hedge.

There were a few pecan trees, but not a villa or an estate to be seen. Instead, ahead of him stretched rows of mobile homes. Singlewide, doublewide, mostly neatly kept and tidy. She took a left onto Beech Crescent and then swung right into Oak Street and pulled in front of a mint green doublewide with crushed white rock landscaping and a flock of plastic geese picking at the stones. Three metal butterflies clung to the siding.

In spite of the kitsch factor, the place was clean and in good repair.

"You grew up here?"

She laughed. "Not hardly." She flipped the trunk and they each hefted a box stamped Lady Bianca. "This is a big step up from where I started out."

She mounted three steps to the porch and then banged the screen door with her hip. "Hey, y'all. I got a delivery," she said, her country accent sounding thicker.

"Comin', honey," a woman called. And then the door opened.

"Hey, Mama," she said, and the two women bussed cheeks over the box.

Luke almost staggered when he saw Toni's mother. Mama made Toni look as conservative as a nun. In fact, the woman was on the flashy side even for Texas. She had hair so blonde it hurt to look at in the glare from the sun, and makeup so heavily applied that it was almost like a second face. Like when a picture is snapped fuzzy and there are two likenesses. She wore a tight pink shirt of some shiny fabric that revealed a hefty amount of cleavage as perfect as two double scoops of vanilla ice cream.

Her jeans were snug and her faux snakeskin boots had decorative spurs.

Her daughter had toned it down a few degrees but when he saw the wink of diamonds on her jeans, he had to think that the apple hadn't fallen far from the gaudy tree.

Mama's eyes lit up and her plump pink lips smiled when she spied him. "You didn't tell me you were bringing a gentleman caller."

"Detective Marciano's with the police, Mama."

"Detective?" She took a step back. "Police?"

"Ms. Diamond is helping us with some inquiries, ma'am."

"So, Toni, you're like a deputy? My, that's so exciting. Just like in the movies. Well, come on in. I've got the coffee on. I can't thank you enough for bringing me those supplies, honey. I don't know what I was thinking, inviting the girls without checking my cosmetics stock first." She twinkled at her daughter. "Good thing I'm your best sales rep."

"You're not. You're my mama and you're holding my daughter hostage. So, you had me over a barrel and you know it."

Her mother laughed, a girlish trill that was, oddly enough, the most genuine thing about her.

Inside, the mobile home was spotless. Full of crap, but all of it clean.

Over the electric fireplace in the living room where another family might have a scenic picture, or a mirror, or a religious symbol, an oil painting of Dolly Parton smiled down at him. At her feet, on the mantel, was a clay pot with a lid and a silver-framed photograph in black and white. Looked like an old wedding picture.

Toni's mother collected Parton mementos the way a dog collected fleas. They were everywhere. A Parton doll in a white angel dress on one table, a collector's plate hanging on one wall and a picture of Mama and Toni with a girl of about ten posing in front of Dollywood on another.

Here You Come Again played softly in the background.

"You're a Dolly Parton fan, I see," he said.

"I sure am. She is a very special lady to me. Our birthday is the same day. A lot of people say we look alike." She struck a pose and cut a glance to her own ample cleavage, and he couldn't stop his lips from twitching.

"The resemblance is remarkable."

"Course, I'm a few years younger, but I always look on Dolly like an older sister. I send her a card on our birthday every year."

"She ever send one back?" another voice joined in. Young, monotone, bored with life. Must be a teenager. Sure enough, an older version of the girl in the Dollywood photo slouched down the hall to the living area and collapsed onto the couch as though the walk had exhausted her.

"Miss Parton is a very busy woman. Naturally, she doesn't have time to write back, but I know she appreciates my cards and on the big birthdays I send a little gift. We don't always do things in order to get something back, missy."

The girl now slumped on the floral sofa fit in with the other two women like a crow would fit into a cage of parrots. He was no expert, but even he was pretty sure her long straight hair was dyed. The black was so heavy it seemed to weigh her down, so her shoulders stooped. In contrast to the hair, her face was unnaturally white, and her makeup looked like she'd applied it with a black Sharpie.

She sported a nose stud but, where he'd have expected a diamond, she had chosen a black bead. She pulled a laptop computer off the table and rested it on her knees. A stack of books with library stickers rested beside it. Simone de Beauvoir, Kant and, for light reading, Stephen King.

Black jeans, black shirt, black and white high tops. Black nail polish that was badly chipped and three silver earrings in the ear he could see, one of which was hanging by a wire. Jaws chomping a wad of gum like it was chewing tobacco.

"And this is my baby, Tiffany," Toni said brightly. "Tiff, this is Detective Marciano."

"Yeah. Tiffany Diamond. Go ahead and arrest my mother for sticking me with a porn star's name."

"I was seventeen years old when you were born and you were my most precious thing. All I knew was that you weren't just a diamond—you were a perfect diamond." She walked over and sat beside her daughter, giving her a one-armed hug. "I couldn't decide between calling you Tiffany or Hope."

He thought, based on what he saw, that Rough might have been a better choice, but he understood that this performance was a set piece; they probably pulled it out whenever somebody new came into their circle.

The daughter groaned theatrically, but she didn't pull out of her mother's embrace. "I can't believe my dad didn't stop you."

The two mothers exchanged a look and Luke got the feeling Mr. Diamond hadn't hung around long enough to give an opinion on the matter.

"Your father loved the name," said Linda Plotnik, shooting Toni a half-pleading, half-warning glance. "He helped your mother pick your pretty name. Anyhow, you know what Dolly says..." Mama practically genuflected before her picture when she mentioned her idol's name."'Decide who you are and then do it on purpose.' Tiffany Diamond is whoever you want her to be."

The girl rolled her eyes.

"Besides, one day you'll get married and then your name won't be remarkable at all."

"And if I follow family tradition that should happen in about a year. Over a shotgun."

CHAPTER 8

Blonde hair, pink lips, good figure, talent and sex—that's all I have to offer.

–Diana Dors

"TIFFANY, honey, you're so smart. You won't make the same mistakes as your mother and me did." Linda's words were confident, but there was a line of worry creasing the makeup on her forehead. "I'll pour the coffee."

She walked to the kitchenette, her boots clacking when she hit the linoleum, and poured three mugs, putting cream and sugar into pots decorated either with ducks or geese, it was hard to tell which. The artist hadn't been much of an ornithologist.

"You want coffee, Tiff?"

"I won't be responsible for deforesting South America and enslaving the people on coffee plantations."

"Guess that's a no."

"I'll get some herbal tea in a minute," Tiffany said, and he thought there was a shred of sheepishness in her tone.

"Looks like some interesting books," he said to her. "You taking summer school?"

"No. I like to read."

"Tiffany's practically a genius," Linda said proudly. "Reads all the time and goes to a gifted class. She knows all kinds of strange things."

The girl slumped lower. If she'd been a turtle she'd have pulled her head all the way into her shell.

"What did you have for breakfast, honey?" Toni asked her daughter.

"I offered her eggs and bacon, but—"

"I'm a vegan."

Linda rolled her eyes. "You can't be a vegan in Texas. It's against the Constitution."

"I had an organic apple in my bag. I ate that."

Linda offered him cream and sugar, both of which he declined. "One of her nicknames is The Iron Butterfly, you know—Dolly Parton. She's a very shrewd businesswoman. She's the secret to my own modest success as a Lady Bianca representative." He noticed now that the big necklace resting on her ample chest was a butterfly. "Why, whenever I'm stuck on something, I just think," here the other two joined in so in three-part harmony he heard, "what would Dolly do?"

The only quote he could recall from Dolly Parton was, "It takes a lot of money to look this cheap." Somehow, he didn't think this was the right moment to bring that up.

While he drank coffee, and Tiffany tapped away at her computer, the two older women opened the boxes of cosmetic supplies and checked off the items inside with a master list. Linda wrote a check, which she gave to her daughter.

When they started carting the stuff down the narrow hallway, he rose and said, "Let me help you with that,"—not entirely to be chivalrous but because he wanted to see more of the business first hand.

"Such a gentleman," Linda said. Not to him, it appeared, but to her daughter. She led them to a bedroom in the mobile home that was lined with deep storage cupboards, all neatly labeled. *Advertising and Marketing Materials*, he read on one, *Eyes, Lips, Cheeks, Skin Care*. She opened a cupboard and started placing eye shadows in custom made compartments with the speed of a seasoned Mahjong player.

"I'm planning to focus on lips," Linda told her daughter.

"Good idea. Start them off with the lip conditioner with SPF 15 and conditioning oils. It's amazing how many women forget to put sunscreen or any kind of moisturizer on their lips. And think how much work they do."

Based on the way these gals could talk, he figured their mouths ought to be worn out by now.

"Then, don't forget the makeup artist's insider tip about putting your foundation on your lips as well as your face. Evens out the tones and provides a nice base for the product to adhere to."

They'd finished with the eye products and were now packing pencils, tubes, and little plastic pots in individual compartments within her *Lips* cupboard.

"Right, I remember. And then outline the lip with pencil."

"Mmm-hmm. Same color as the lipstick you're going to choose. Then fill in with the lipstick, and you can highlight the center of the lower lip with a swipe of glittery gloss, or go over the entire lip with one of the sheer shimmering glosses."

"How many is that?"

Toni grinned. "Five products for one pair of lips. Not bad. And your gals will look so gorgeous they'll have to buy them all."

"Plus, some of the girls already told me they're running low on the eye products from my last party."

"Good. Make sure you display all the new eye colors. The palette for fall is really pretty."

He started opening cabinets and found each of them packed with stuff. "I thought you were short on stock."

"I was."

"How many women are you expecting at this party of yours? There's a ton of stuff in here."

"But not in every color. The secret is to be well stocked so that when a client needs a raspberry sherbet lip gloss you have one. What always happens to me is that I've got a dozen strawberry shortcake lip glosses but I'm fresh out of the raspberry. You see, Detective, I operate like a store, only without the expense of rent and staff.

"My customers don't want to wait for me to order their products; they want me to have items available for them at any time. That's why I needed Toni to stock me up before my *Love your Lips* party." She turned to Toni. "Wait 'til I show you the invitations. They're shaped like kisses. When I saw them I knew I had to have the party. It was a sign."

"Stevie next door wanted to know why I was throwing a Valentine's Day party in July. Honestly, if brains were grease that woman wouldn't have enough to slick the head of a pin."

He recalled the check writing. "And you have to buy all this stuff up front?"

"Exactly like a store. I buy at wholesale and sell at retail, which gives me a very nice fifty percent profit on all my sales."

He opened all the cupboards except the one marked *Men* because, frankly, he didn't want to know.

"Where are the sample packs you give out when you do a makeover?"

"*Advertising and Marketing*."

He opened the cupboard. Inside, along with poster board glossies of faces that looked as though they belonged at a display booth, and boxes of brochures, business cards, and catalogs, he found four varieties of the same sample pack that had been beside the dead woman when she'd been found.

Toni left what she was doing and came up beside him. "Here's what I was talking about. We've got sample packs in different shades to complement a client's coloring. These are the ones for this year." She raised her voice, "Mama, do you have any of the sample packs from last year?"

"Goodness, no, honey. Why would I have those? They're no good anymore."

Toni raised her eyebrows at him. "See? No rep with an ounce of integrity is going to give out old ones."

He rubbed his thumb along the edge of the plastic package. Even mass produced, they had to cost a buck or two a pop. "Do the reps have to buy those?"

"Of course."

"Marketing must cost a ton."

"Cost of doing business, Detective. You get out of an enterprise what you put into it."

Or invested your hard-earned money in a lot of colored junk you couldn't sell. He supposed it was, as Toni would no doubt tell him, all about attitude.

The three of them headed back down the hallway to the main living area.

"How about staying for lunch, honey? I've got some fruit salad and I can rustle up—"

"We can't stay. I'm going to miss a session as it is, and Detective Marciano has a murder to solve."

"Murder?" Her mother dropped the happy face, and he saw Toni's lips move, no doubt as she swore silently at herself. He didn't think she'd intended to tell her mom there'd been a murder—though she was being naïve if she thought it wouldn't be in all the papers and on the local TV.

"Who was murdered?" Linda Plotnik glanced at him, "And what does Toni have to do with it?"

"Nothing, Mama. It's nothing to do with me. The woman had had a Lady Bianca makeover, that's all, and the police want to know all about our business in case there's a connection." She turned to him. "Even though there isn't one."

Linda Plotnik did not look relieved. "I never watch the news or read the papers if I can help it. Too negative. But—" She put a hand to her chest. "Oh, my. A woman involved in Lady Bianca was murdered? I hope you're looking after my girl, Detective."

"Yes, ma'am."

She turned to Toni, a worried expression pulling her eyebrows together. "And don't you go putting your nose in things that are none of your business."

"I won't."

Ignoring her daughter, she turned back to Luke. "She does, you know. Nosy. That's what she is. Always has been from the time she was no bigger than a June bug."

"Can we talk about something else?"

"Are you a married man, Detective?"

"Not that!"

"Well, it's the other subject I'm interested in. You bring a nice looking man around to my house and I get to wondering."

"Mother," Toni said in a warning tone. "Detective Marciano is here on business."

Those baby blue doll's eyes widened. "I'm thinking about business. He could have a wife, girlfriend, mother, sisters, all kinds of future Lady Bianca customers. You don't know until you ask."

Luke felt sizzles of emotion running through the atmosphere. Toni's cheeks were pink with embarrassment. Linda, unabashed, was clearly checking him out. And from the kid he picked up pure, unadulterated humiliation to be stuck in this trailer with these people.

"I'm divorced," he finally said. "And I don't think I'll be

buying my ex-wife makeup any time soon. Sisters and mother live too far away. But thanks."

"Toni's divorced, too."

"Mama!"

"In case you were wondering."

"Did you bring my eyeliners?" Tiffany asked her mother.

"Yes. Glad you reminded me." She hefted her purse and pulled out a quartet of black pencils.

"Cool."

"And be good for Grandma. She's really excited about you helping with the party."

"Whatever."

While Toni had a few words with her daughter, the mother sidled up to him not looking at all abashed at being caught out in some of the most heavy-handed matchmaking he'd ever witnessed. "Don't mind me. I want to see her happy, is all."

"I don't mind."

"I have no patience for subtlety." Like that was news. He had a shrewd idea she bullied her friends into buying makeup.

She looked at him with eyes that reminded him of Toni's. "You're a good man. I can tell these things. I'm a lot smarter than I look, you know."

"I know." He leaned closer, so he could see each individual platinum curl and the smell of hairspray caught in the back of his throat. "So's your daughter."

She laughed aloud at that and patted him on the shoulder. "I hope I see you again."

"Good-bye, Mother," Toni said, before he could answer. Which he figured was just as well.

"SORRY ABOUT THAT," Toni said as soon as they were back on the road. "I thought you being a cop might intimidate my mama. Seems I was wrong."

"Don't be hard on her. I like your mom."

"Truth is, I like her too." She sighed. "And one day, I hope my daughter will like me again." She glanced over at him. "Do you have kids?"

"No. Never got around to it."

They were silent for a few minutes as the highway rolled beneath them. "You told Mama you've got a mom and sisters, is that true?"

"Sure. I grew up in a big, Italian, Catholic family. I'm the baby with three older sisters who all bossed me around."

"Wow, you seem so tough to be from an all girl family."

"Having three older sisters is what made me tough."

She laughed. "What about your father?"

"He's been gone three years, now. He was an auto mechanic. Took the business over from his father and wanted me to take over from him. But I knew from way back I wanted to be a cop."

"So, the business closed?"

He shook his head, looking amused. "*Marciano & Sons* is now run by Maria Marciano, the oldest. He got such a kick out of that."

"You help her out sometimes?"

"Why do you ask?"

"Your hands. You've got a trace of grease under your nails and the skin is cracking, from harsh cleaners, I bet."

He glanced down at his hands ruefully. "I remodel old trucks. It's a hobby, specially when I can't sleep. I was working on one last night."

"Lady Bianca has a nice cuticle cream that should help with the dry skin and prevent that cracking."

He chuckled. "You never give up, do you?"

"Don't worry. I promise not to sell you anything. This is a present."

She could feel him looking at her. "I want to ask you something and I don't want you to take it the wrong way," Marciano said to her.

She glanced up at him. "Whoa. Now I'm on my guard. Is this how you interrogate your prisoners? 'I'm going to ask you some tough questions but I don't want you to take them the wrong way?'"

He met her gaze. "Depends on the prisoner."

The highway rolled beneath them with a shushing sound.

"So, what do you want to ask me that I might take the wrong way?"

"You're smart. What are you doing shilling makeup door to door?"

"And here I thought you were going to ask me about my political affiliations or my religious beliefs." She sighed. "This is not the first time I've been asked this question. I love what I do. I like helping a woman bring out her unique beauty. Every face is a new possibility. A blank canvas if you like."

"Hope you're more of a Gainsborough than a Picasso," he muttered, making her snort with laughter.

"I thought you of all people would understand."

"You thought I would understand selling makeup?"

"In a way, we're in the same business you and I."

"Come again?" If she'd grabbed his revolver and shot him with it he couldn't have looked more shocked.

"Think about it. We both try to clean up the world's ugliness and make it a better place."

He hit her with his steeliest glance. "I'm a cop. I fight crime."

"How much of your day is spent on paperwork and bureaucracy? Boring meetings and community relations?"

"More than I'd like," he admitted. "But that's got nothing to do with my question."

He was so serious looking, and yet there was a sizzle of something behind his eyes that suggested this man strapped on his tough cop persona every morning along with his gun holster. She knew all about assuming an identity. She did it every morning, too.

"You know that expression 'dirt poor'?"

"Sure."

"Well, I lived it. My daddy was a two-bit rodeo rider when he met Mama. By the time I was born, he was already out West trying to break into the movies. He had a bit part in a Spaghetti Western, and I guess he thought he was headed for the big time. But Westerns were in decline and he was a bowlegged country boy who didn't know how to do much but talk Texan and ride a bronco. He stuck it out for a while, doing stunts and eking out a living. But not enough to send us any money. So we lived with my mom's folks and let me tell you, a Pentecostal preacher in a town where folks were poor was even poorer. If somebody gave him a few dollars for marrying them or something, you know what he'd do?"

"What?"

"He'd find somebody worse off to share the wealth with. And he really had to look hard to find anybody poorer than us. But they were good people, and they loved Mama and me even though she'd fallen from the path of righteousness, and I was the living proof."

"It's hard to picture you dirt poor."

"Well, I was. We didn't have a TV. I used to sneak to my friend Jo-Jo's house and watch reruns of *Dallas* and *Dynasty*. That was the life I knew I wanted. I fell in love right then and there with glamorous people and clothes, and I vowed to myself that I was gonna be one of 'em. Them." She shook her head. "I get talking about the old days and I start talking white trash, which was the official language of my childhood."

"Looks like you got your wish."

"Yes, sir, I did. I got it by working hard and selling a product

I believe in. I've also helped a goodly number of women set up their own independent businesses. I'm real proud of my team."

"You're selling me, all right. But everybody in your organization isn't as ethical as you are. I checked out some websites."

The look she sent him was far from apologetic. "Lady Bianca is a big organization. Sometimes the wrong people join up. Are you going to tell me that every police officer in the country is perfect, law abiding and honest?"

His face registered surprise as he glanced at her. It was a look she'd been getting since she'd first grown breasts and dyed her hair blonde. The kind of look Marilyn Monroe might have received if she'd opened her mouth and expounded a new theory of quantum physics.

"I take your point."

She accelerated smoothly around a U-Haul truck. "I help women look better, and that makes them feel good about themselves. If you ask me, happy people have less reason to commit crime."

"Oh, come on."

"Look, I'm not pretending I can cure cancer or solve world hunger or fix that whole global warming thing. But if I make someone feel better about themselves, maybe that gives them a little more confidence to get out there and do those things. We are also a very green company," she told him. "I'm sure you noticed the minimal packaging, no extra boxes or cellophane and every one of our containers is recyclable. And, as I keep telling Tiffany, we also use natural ingredients grown and harvested in a sustainable manner."

"It would be greener if everybody stopped wearing makeup."

She glanced at him from under her lashes. "Now you're just being silly."

CHAPTER 9

I have always a sacred veneration for anyone I observe to be a little out of repair in his person, as supposing him either a poet or a philosopher.

–Jonathan Swift

"WELL, I'LL BE," Luke said as they walked into the hotel to find the day's electronic message board had changed. The Lady Bianca convention still held top billing, but the area toastmasters were gone. In their place were two new groups—a medical equipment sales seminar in the Getty Ballroom and, lo and behold, Mystery Readers of America registration and opening banquet in the Cactus Room.

Toni paused beside him. "A mystery readers' convention. What do you bet Violet was here to attend that?" Satisfaction spiked like a tiny fist punching the air, *Yes!*

He nodded, still staring at the board.

"It makes sense that she was a bookworm. She looked like a

teacher or librarian, didn't she? The clothes, the Birkenstocks, the ink between her fingers. And she named herself after a Holmes character."

He stuck his hand in his pocket and jingled the change in there. "Then the bookworm had a makeover. She said it was because she had a date."

"Which suggests she was trying to impress. First date, maybe."

She cast her mind back to the image of the woman's dead body on the gurney and the picture came through as clear as though she'd snapped a photo.

"She wasn't wearing a wedding ring, unless that Celtic design was one, which I doubt."

"Think I'll check out the Cactus Room."

"Sorry you wasted your time today," she said, feeling anything but sorry. She was still sad the poor woman had been murdered but it was nice to be proven right. The death had nothing to do with Lady Bianca and they could all get back to their seminar.

"Oh," he said, letting his espresso gaze settle on her for a warm moment, "It wasn't a waste."

And he was gone.

Which was just as well since she was, for the first time in years, speechless.

LUKE STRODE into the Cactus Room and knew he wasn't in Lady Bianca land anymore. Not a sequin, a sash or a single balloon could he find in the sparsely populated conference room. No dress code either unless the requirements were tweed, knit sweaters, and eyeglasses.

Where the Lady Bianca crowd tended to display cosmetics and prizes everywhere, usually with a lot of purple frills and glitzy helium balloons wafting along for the ride, the mystery readers went in for books. Tables stacked with books. Hardcover, paperback, and trade paperback. Hefty, glossy bestsellers written by household names and obscure, small-press titles whose print run was probably in the hundreds.

The bookworms who had registered wandered around, some with their name tags already hanging around their necks, holding simple cloth bags printed with the words "A Conference to Die For." The logo was a laughing skull.

In Jane Doe's case those words were more prescient than the conference organizers could have imagined.

He headed first for the long table at the front of the room where three registrars sat: two ladies who had to be in their seventies, grandmotherly types with white hair and glasses, and a skinny young man, intense and scraggly in a black sweater vest. College student, Luke guessed.

Both the young guy and one of the older women were occupied with registrations, but the other woman put down her Kindle when he stepped in front of her, and eyed him with a smiling welcome.

"Here to register?"

"I'm a police officer." He backed up so she could see his belt badge and sidearm, then introduced himself. "I've got a few questions."

Her expression was a cross between amusement and concern. "We only read about crime, Detective. We aren't planning any."

"There's already been a murder in the hotel."

Her hand went to her heart and he wished he hadn't been so blunt. "But—I didn't—I've been so busy, traveling straight here and then coming down to help with the registration that I never listened to the news. Oh, how awful. What happened?"

"A woman was stabbed to death. I think she might have been with your group." He pulled out the photograph. "Do you recognize this woman?"

The lady adjusted her glasses more firmly on her nose and gazed at the photograph for a long time, long enough that he began to hope she had recognized the dead woman. Finally, she said, "It's so sad to see them die young. One of my nieces died tragically. Drug overdose. I remember the viewing. How pale she looked and how peaceful. This reminds me —a little."

"I'm sorry to upset you. Do you need some water?"

"No. I'm fine." She blinked hard. "Just for that moment..."

"Any chance you recognize the woman in the picture?"

"No. I'm sorry. I've never seen her before." She handed back the photo.

"How many do you expect at the convention?"

"About a hundred and fifty. And then the speakers and authors on top of that. But our members come from all over the country. I don't know them all."

He repeated the process with the other two at the registration desk and struck out twice more.

"So, none of you registered her."

"No," said the young guy, "but registration didn't start 'til today. There's always a few who come early to check out the city or hook up with friends." He shrugged. "Maybe she arrived early."

The second woman said, "There are other conferences here, Detective, as I'm sure you're aware. Perhaps she's with Lady Bianca."

Funny how every conference wanted to shunt the murder victim to somebody else's agenda. "In fact, she did have a Lady Bianca makeover yesterday. She put her name on the customer card as Violet Hunter. What do you make of that?"

"*The Adventure of the Copper Beeches,*" the first woman said with a fond smile. "Not Conan Doyle's greatest work, perhaps, but always a favorite of mine."

"The fact that she chose a name out of a Holmes story

makes this conference a likely bet. When do you expect everyone to have registered?"

"Not until tomorrow sometime."

"Any way of finding out who came in early?"

"Yes. Everyone who registered used a special code to get the conference rate with the hotel. The front desk should have that information."

"Thanks. Mind if I look around?"

"Of course not, Detective. And if you care to purchase any of the books, in most cases the authors are here at the convention and would be happy to sign them for you."

He nodded and turned to check out the readers milling around the book-laden tables. What kind of people came to a conference like this? He'd always loved mysteries but he couldn't imagine ever wanting to hang out with other people who read them. He'd never considered reading a group activity.

He'd assumed a book club was a commercial enterprise that sold novels at a discount—until a former girlfriend had set him straight. Thursday nights once a month were sacred; her book club night. And he soon learned that the Monday, Tuesday, and Wednesday leading up to the Thursday night were sacrosanct too, since she was always behind and had to read the book in a hurry to be ready to discuss it.

It seemed the book club had gone a step further. Now there were entire conventions devoted to mystery reading. He wondered how many books these poor suckers had to cram in before they got here.

"Is that disdainful smile directed at me, young man?"

Something about the voice made him straighten and wipe the smirk right off his mouth. "No, ma'am," he said, and found himself confronting an elderly woman who couldn't have been more than five feet tall. Her ample bosom stuck out from her chest like a shelf, and he imagined her resting her novel there while she was reading.

She had a thick head of red curly hair that had to be a wig, and wore clip-on earrings of cascading fruits that reminded him of Carmen Miranda's headdresses. Her lipstick was bright red, but a different red than the hair, and under turquoise eyelids, that looked as though they'd been painted on by a toddler with a crayon, a pair of sharp gray eyes snapped with humor. "You here for the conference? You don't seem the type."

"No. I'm not. Are you?"

She cackled with laughter. Big teeth stained with nicotine and coffee. "Yes, I am, and I'm exactly the type: an old spinster without enough to do." She had the raspy tones of a smoker. He bet her doctor had been nagging her for years to quit.

She'd been eyeing his badge and sidearm but he still told her he was a cop and pulled out his wallet ID before she could demand to see it. Somehow he knew she would. She studied it carefully before asking what he wanted.

He showed her the photograph and once more was disappointed after she studied it carefully, pulling on the reading glasses hanging around her neck to do so, and then shaking her head.

"What kind of people *do* come to the conference?" he asked her.

"Folks like me. Teachers or retired teachers. Writers, of course, and people from every walk of life who love the genre and want to know more about it. We get some young people, but most of us are middle-aged or older. We're the ones with the most time to read and the most money to spend indulging our whims."

"Were you here last night?"

"No. I flew in this morning from Boston. Just got here an hour ago and came down to register—and browse the books."

Her gaze strayed behind him to a stack of shiny new hardcovers. He turned to follow her gaze. "Perfect Murder," he read aloud. "A novel?"

"No. Non-fiction. Joe's a true-crime writer. I understand he spent several years researching this book."

"Great. Exactly what cops need. A textbook on how to murder people and get away with it." He picked up the book and skimmed the back cover copy.

"You can tell the author exactly what you think of him and his book," the gravelly voice informed him with relish. "He just walked in."

Luke's first thought was that the guy heading their way did not fit the profile as described to him by his new friend. Joseph Mandeville, author of *Perfect Murder*, sported a manly, chiseled chin, wavy black hair that was exactly the length to scream "artiste" and big, greedy lips. He had a large body, as though he'd played a lot of sports in his younger days, but his time behind the computer had softened him. He wore jeans, cowboy boots that had never seen the range, a black corduroy jacket, and a gray patterned scarf draped nonchalantly around his neck.

After pausing inside the doorway, he glanced around and when his gaze lighted on his own books, he headed toward them without the pretense of being interested in any other book in the room but the one he'd penned.

"Joe," said the old woman beside him, stepping forward, "I'm Helen Barnes. We met last year in Knoxville. I moderated the panel discussion on strangling methods."

"Of course, Helen, how are you?" Joseph Mandeville reached forward and kissed both of her withered cheeks with European aplomb.

"I'm fine, thank you. This is Detective Marciano. He's interested in your book."

"Of course. My pleasure." And the author reached into his pocket and pulled out a fountain pen. "Whom do I make it out to?"

"Don't need it signed, thanks. I'd like to ask you a couple of questions though."

The author held up his hands and raised his voice in mock alarm. "I never give away my sources or my secrets."

Pretentious ass. "I'm investigating a murder, here at the hotel. When did you arrive?"

The man blinked. "A murder? Here? Really? I was in my room writing. I never looked at the news. Who's the victim?"

"We're trying to find that out, sir. When did you arrive?"

"Day before yesterday. I had a couple of book signings and a speaking engagement before the conference started."

"And you're staying in the hotel?"

"Yes." He glanced at Helen Barnes and licked his greedy lips. "Can't believe no one told me there'd been a murder right under my nose. I'll have to call my agent. Maybe write an article for one of the big magazines." As though a violent death were a big treat he'd missed, and an employment opportunity.

Once more Luke drew out the photograph of the dead woman. "Do you recognize her?"

The artiste façade slipped for a second and Luke watched Mandeville's eyes widen in genuine shock. He reached out for the picture, then stopped. "Oh my God. I know her. Her name is Amy Neuman. But—"

"Are you sure?"

His gaze stayed riveted on the photograph and his upper lip looked suddenly clammy. "Of course I'm sure. I had dinner with her Sunday night."

CHAPTER 10

No woman makes herself up for a man. She does it for herself. But if a man notices, that's always nice.

–Lady Bianca

"I CAN'T BELIEVE Amy's dead," Joseph Mandeville said, shoving a hand through his hair so it fell in romantic disarray. Marciano wondered how he'd look with a prison regulation buzz cut.

"Murdered, in fact. Something you are quite an expert on." He and Henderson were in Mandeville's suite sharing the space with the man's laptop, his two cell phones, his cloying cologne, and his oversized ego. He'd called Henderson and asked him to come along as he interviewed the author.

"I didn't kill her. Why on earth would I?"

Marciano opened the hardcover Mandeville was here to promote and read the opening words of the book. "The perfect murder needs no reason. That's why it's perfect."

"Come on. I get paid to create an impression. Doesn't mean I believe that nonsense."

Marciano glanced over at Henderson, who smoothly took over. "How did you meet Ms. Neuman?"

"She emailed me through my website, originally."

"Where did she live?"

Mandeville opened his big lips and then pursed them as though thinking. "Seattle, I believe."

They already had the woman's registration information from the front desk and knew she was from Seattle.

"And you live in New York."

"Right. That's the beauty of technology. It's made the planet the size of one's office or living room."

"When did Ms. Neuman contact you?"

"About a year ago. It was right after Killer Teens came out. That's a true crime about teen-aged murderers. She wanted to use a section of the book as a teaching exercise for her sophomore English class, and wrote to ask my permission."

"Did you give it?"

"Sure. If a few of those kids bought one of my books it would be worth it. I looked on it as free publicity."

"When I was a sophomore we studied Macbeth," Marciano said.

Mandeville smiled dutifully. "My books are as gory but more contemporary. And there are plenty of tragedies in high school. Anyway, she said she was a fan of my work and we began corresponding by email. When it turned out we were both coming to this conference, we decided to meet for dinner."

"Whose idea was the dinner?"

"Mine, I think."

"And was it your idea that she come in before the conference started? Before there was anybody around?"

Mandeville's eyes flashed with annoyance but he kept his tone calm. "She'd already decided to come in early. She'd never been to Texas and wanted to do some sightseeing while she was here."

The weight of two police officers staring at him seemed to unnerve him. "Oh, for God's sake. If I wanted to murder a woman I barely know, I'd hardly have done it in the hotel where we're both staying, after we spent the evening together. I'm not a fool."

"Where did you go for dinner?"

"A gourmet steak house." He shrugged. "When in Rome. I wanted to show her some real Texas fun."

"Had you ever met before?"

He glanced toward the window where a plane arrowed slowly across the hazy sky. "Maybe we passed each other at a conference in the past. Who knows?"

"What did you talk about over dinner?"

He opened his hands the way lecturers do when making a point. "Books, of course. Writing. Teaching. Her life, my life." He stretched out his legs in front of him, but Marciano thought he was trying too hard to convey the idea that he was relaxed.

"She seemed upset about something. Her cell phone rang a few times during dinner. She checked the number once and then put the thing on vibrate, but I could tell she was edgy. You know? She was sitting with her back to the window, but a couple of times she turned around to check outside. It didn't seem like she was people-watching."

Henderson made a careful note. "You think someone was following her? Harassing her?"

"I don't know. I asked her if everything was okay and she said it was."

"What time did you leave the restaurant?"

"Around ten, I think."

"Did that Texas fun continue when you got back to the hotel?" Marciano asked.

Mandeville jerked to his feet and stalked to the window,

standing there with his back to them. "No. She was going through a difficult time. She's—she was in the process of getting a divorce. She wasn't ready to move on."

"So you didn't put the moves on her?"

"Of course I did." He spun around and snapped, "I'm a red-blooded unattached male staying in a deluxe hotel room with a king-sized bed. I suggested we come back to my place for a nightcap."

He actually said *nightcap*.

"And she refused?"

Under Henderson's steady, unmoving gaze, Mandeville's shifted until he was staring at the tasteful floral print on the wall. "Yes."

"How did her rejection make you feel?" Henderson asked in his emotionless way.

"I didn't feel like killing her because she turned me down," he snapped. "I'm not that desperate for a woman."

"So, if you have nothing to hide, you won't mind if we look around?"

Mandeville stared at him and Luke figured the guy'd done enough research that he must know they didn't have enough articulable facts to justify a warrant. But, if he was as innocent as he claimed, the easiest way to prove it was to let them paw through his sock drawer.

Mandeville blinked first. "Fine. Just don't make a mess."

Henderson held out one of the preprinted consent forms and asked Mandeville to sign it, which he did with an angry flourish of his fountain pen.

"What do you figure?" Marciano asked Henderson when they left Mandeville's suite.

"Would have been nice to find a blood-stained knife."

"Yeah. You know, I agree with him. He's too smart to kill a woman he ate dinner with and do it right in the hotel where they're both staying."

"He's arrogant. I think he'd do about anything for publicity." Marciano punched the down button on the elevator. "He's got his next book already. *The Night my Pen Pal was Murdered.*"

"You think he killed her to sell a few books?"

Luke shrugged.

"Seemed like he wanted to be helpful."

"Too helpful. You buy the mysterious cell phone calls and her checking over her shoulder?"

"Now we know who she is, we can get hold of her cell phone records. I'll get onto that."

Marciano nodded. "Better let Seattle PD know. They'll have to inform next of kin. I'll check the restaurant. Double-check her last movements. Try to follow some kind of trail."

Henderson's cell phone rang. He answered and had a brief conversation.

"They were able to squeeze the autopsy in today at three."

"Great. Meet you back here at two-thirty."

Marciano headed out of the hotel, pulling his sunglasses on as he went.

Not far past the revolving door to the main entrance, a couple of enterprising teens were selling two-inch campaign-style buttons in purple printed with the words *NO, I Don't want a Lady Bianca makeover*. From the brisk sales, he had to think everyone in the area had been approached by more than one eager sales rep.

He'd barely stepped off the hotel property when he saw several groups of Lady Bianca types heading his way. Already, he could spot them, all those skirts and pumps. The third group he passed contained the most Lady Bianca of all the reps

—Toni Diamond, her sunglasses sparkling in the light. He'd have nodded and kept going, but she stopped him.

"Detective," she said, detaching herself from her group and walking over to him. "I'm so happy to see you." She gestured to the group behind her, all looking at her like fledgling chicks watching Mother Hen. "We were practicing some friendly fishing."

He gestured to the button sellers. "Doesn't look like you're catching much."

The sun glinted off her diamond-studded glasses when she shook her head. "You'd be surprised. It's fun to encourage new customers to try our products. And a little bit of resistance is good for training purposes."

"Well, I've got some fishing of my own to do, if you'll excuse me."

"Of course. I know you've got police business to attend to, but I've got something for you."

She reached into her bag and pulled out a tube, offering it to him.

He didn't take it immediately. "It's purple."

"Don't be a chauvinist. It's lilac and it's the hand moisturizer and cuticle cream I was telling you about."

She lifted his hand and placed the tube on his palm, giving both a little pat. "I talked to one of our reps whose husband is a mechanic. He swears by the stuff. She said you should rub this all over your hands and under your nails before you work on greasy engines. It prevents the dirt from sticking. Then, after you clean up, rub the cream in well." She mimed the process on her own fingers. "Especially around the sides where the skin gets dry and cracked."

"I don't—"

"No need to thank me." She twinkled at him. "Maybe you'll love the cream so much you'll recommend it to your sister. Bye now," she said in her eternally sunny way and was gone.

He probably would, he thought. He'd started out investigating a murder and he'd end up pimping makeup to his relatives, God help him.

As he walked away he heard a burst of feminine laughter and some excited chatter. He had to stifle a grin as he stuffed the lilac tube in his pocket. That woman had friendly fished him, hook, line, and sinker.

The walk to the steak house Mandeville directed him to took him less than ten minutes when he deliberately held his pace to a stroll.

The restaurant was a mid-priced steak house. Lots of dark wood and blue gingham café curtains across big windows. The lunch crowd was thinning out, but the hostess offered him a practiced smile and a quick glance behind him before asking, "Lunch for one?"

He slipped her his card. "I'm investigating a crime. I'd like to ask a few questions about a couple who had dinner here Sunday night."

"I wasn't working Sunday. Any idea who their server was?"

"No. But they sat by the window."

"Probably Candy then. Or Ken." She bit her lip as though not quite sure how to proceed then said, "Right this way. I'll seat you and bring the server to you."

"Thanks." Since she dropped a menu in front of him, he opened it and studied a list of steaks, ribs, and chicken dishes, depicted in both glowing prose and vivid, mouth-watering photographs.

"You were asking about one of my customers?" a female voice asked.

"That's right. Candy?"

She nodded. Candy was a plump woman on the dark side of forty with short blonde hair that was longer on one side than the other.

After he introduced himself, he said, "Can I talk to you for a few minutes?"

"Sure." She seemed more than happy to sit down and join him.

Their waitress approached. "Do you want to order anything?"

"I'll take a couple of the steak sandwiches to go."

"Sure thing."

"And whatever Candy would like?"

"Could you bring a couple of iced teas for right now, Lisa?" Candy added. The way the other waitress nodded and headed off to do her bidding suggested Candy was liked, or at least respected, by the other staff.

He placed two pictures on the table. One was Mandeville's publicity photo that he'd sliced from the book jacket with his penknife, and the other was the photo of the dead woman, Amy Neuman. "Did you serve either of these people dinner Sunday night?"

"Yeah, I remember them. They had dinner at Table 25. In the window there." She touched Amy's picture with a red fingertip. "What happened to her?"

The iced tea came, real stuff, dark with tannins. Lisa placed two big glasses clinking with ice on the table and set out sugar and lemon.

"Thanks, hon," Candy said.

"Welcome." After a curious glance at the pictures, Lisa headed off with her empty tray.

"She was murdered. Sunday night. We're trying to figure out who did it and why."

Candy's eyes were a faded blue, but the concern in them was sharp. "She was killed right after she ate dinner here? Lord, that's tragic. She seemed so nice."

"You must serve a lot of customers in a night. You've got a good memory."

She smiled briefly. "A good memory is a real asset to a waitress. I haven't needed to write an order down in thirty years. Besides, those two were hard to forget. They were fighting."

He pulled out his notebook. "What about?"

"I didn't hear much, obviously, but you can always tell when customers aren't getting along." She sighed. "I don't know why everybody thinks they have to do their breaking up in public. It's a lie that anybody acts more civilized in a restaurant, believe me. I've been hit with flying food, wine, water, even had to help restrain a woman who went after her husband with one of the steak knives one time."

"Were the two at Table 25 violent?"

"No. Not them. But that woman barely ate a bite of her food, mostly pushed it around on her plate. And it was the rib-eye and scampi platter, too. A specialty of the house. Everybody loves that dish." Candy shook her head. "Didn't even take the rest to go."

"And they were definitely fighting?"

"They bickered, then would break off when I got near. Too bad, because they came in like a pair of lovebirds. Holding hands and all."

"Really?" He glanced up at her. "Do you think they were intimate?"

"Sleeping together, you mean?" She glanced back at Table 25, now empty and awaiting its next drama. "Oh, yeah."

He began to feel a lot more interested in the author. "What time did they leave?"

"I can find out when he left exactly. He paid the bill by credit card. It would be time and date stamped. She ran out ten minutes earlier."

"They didn't leave together?"

"No. Like I said, they were fighting. She left first. Pretty upset, too."

. . .

HENDERSON WAS SLIPPING his cell phone into his pocket when Marciano tracked him down in Longhorn B. He accepted the wrapped steak sandwich with a brief nod. "Amy got some calls that night. All from her husband's cell phone."

"She was married?"

"Mandeville was right. She'd filed for divorce."

He sat down at the conference table, unwrapped his own sandwich and took a bite. "How many calls?"

"Four between the hours of eight and ten p.m."

"They stopped before she died. Interesting. None since?"

"Nope. And it gets better. Guess where the husband is?"

Marciano stopped mid-chew. "Here?" At Henderson's nod, he banged his fist softly against the fake oak boardroom table. "How long's he been in town?"

Henderson's expression didn't change, but then it rarely did. "He got here Sunday."

"Where do we find him?"

"The Best Western. Three blocks away."

"Anybody told him yet about his wife?"

"They're leaving that to us."

Not that he ever liked delivering this kind of news, but if the guy had murdered his wife, it wouldn't be news and they'd be able to watch his reactions. "Good."

"What did you find out?"

"Mandeville lied to us," he said. "Waitress at the restaurant said he and Amy came in all over each other and then had a big fight. Amy left alone. The waitress said he paid the bill and followed about ten minutes later. I've got a copy of the bill. It's time-stamped. 9:12 p.m."

Henderson took a bite of his sandwich, chewed reflectively. "Maybe the ex didn't like that she was having an affair."

"Mandeville said she started writing to him a year ago. Wonder when they started sleeping together?"

"And how the husband felt about it."

"After the autopsy, how about we pay Amy's husband a call?"

CHAPTER 11

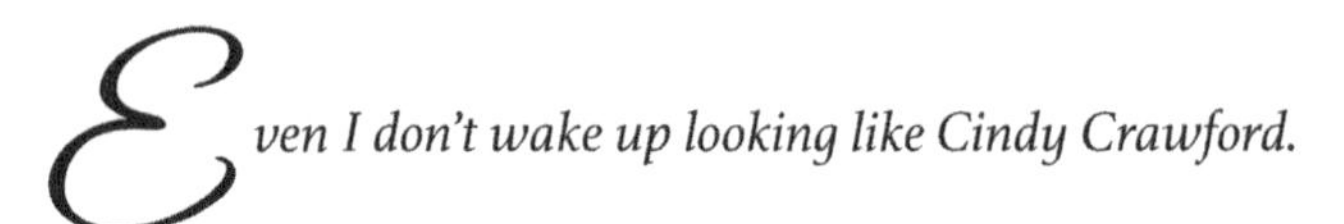

Even I don't wake up looking like Cindy Crawford.

–Cindy Crawford

"YOUR TWO BEST FRIENDS," Toni announced, standing at the front of the seminar room and holding up a glass of water in her left hand and a signature mauve tube in her right. She thought of how horrified Luke had been when she'd handed him a colored tube and found even more fuel for her smile.

"Water and daytime moisturizer with sunscreen." She made a cheers motion with the water, sipped to make her point, and put it down on the table beside her.

"I mean it. The best moisturizer is water. You should drink at least eight glasses a day."

She heard a theatrical groan from a preppy looking gal in the front row who couldn't be more than twenty-two. "Water tastes boring."

"I find a little added lemon or cucumber makes it easy to

drink. If you don't have lemon, use a squirt of the lemon concentrate. Try replacing a couple of cups of coffee with herbal tea. You'll sell more skincare products when your own skin is glowing and radiant. Trust me on this. And it's good to remind your clients, too, that they should be drinking water."

"Or juice?"

"Sure. But not soda. In summer or after you've been on a plane or in air-conditioned buildings like this one, the air is super dry. A couple of extra glasses will help moisturize your skin from the inside. In fact," she paused to look out over the room. "There are definitely a few tired and dehydrated faces out there. At the back of the room you'll find a handy ice water station and lots of glasses. Go ahead. Help yourselves."

About half the women stood and headed for the back of the room. A few waved water bottles around so she could see they were hydrating in their own fashion.

She took another sip of water and put the glass down again. "Now, sunscreen. Winter, summer, wear it. You're looking for a minimum SPF of 15 for daily wear. You know what you should wear at the beach?"

"SPF 30?" her preppy friend shouted out. She held up her water so Toni would see she'd listened.

"Wrong. Stay away from the beach!" She grinned at them. "It was a trick question. If you insist on going to the beach, wear SPF 45 plus a hat and cover-up. Nothing ages our skin faster than the sun.

"As you all know, Lady Bianca daytime moisturizers all contain sunscreen. Don't forget to apply it to the back of your neck if you wear your hair short and the tops of your ears if they are exposed to the elements. Of course, you should always have sunscreen on your lips. If your lipstick or gloss doesn't already contain it, use our patented lip balm. To moisturize, plump, and protect."

Her skincare basics class held about fifty reps. Some new to the company, some looking for a refresher course. Or a chance to sit quietly for fifty minutes. She went through the full range of products for dry skin, oily skin, combination skin, sensitive skin, and aging skin.

A Halle Berry look-alike in a pale blue suit raised her hand. "Do you have any suggestions for puffy eyes?"

"Puffy eyes are annoying and make you look tired. Usually because you are tired, it's why your eyes are puffy in the first place." She stopped to sip more water. "First you want to bring the puffiness down. In the morning or late afternoon before you go out for the evening. Good old cucumber slices work great. So do cold, wet tea bags. Regular tea is fine. But I like chamomile. Of course, you're going to brew a pot of chamomile tea and drink it. Great for the skin and very relaxing."

"Now, while you're stretched out for five or ten minutes with your eyes shut don't be thinking you need to waste that time. You can put on a motivational tape, you can dream up ways to increase your sales or you can practice visualizing yourself wearing a tiara and accepting whatever prize you are working toward at the annual Lady Bianca convention's closing banquet."

She held her right hand in the air, palm toward herself. "I bet you can guess what prize I visualize winning." She waggled her ring finger. "I've got the spot all ready for my two-carat diamond ring. Can we all visualize it?"

There was a spurt of laughter and some applause. It was an open secret that she and Nicole were neck and neck for the division sales title. Again. "If any of you ladies would like to order some product from me before month end, I'd be happy to take your order," she teased.

More laughter.

"Okay, back to our relaxing eye treatment. Five or ten minutes later you rinse with cool water, pat the area dry and then apply your eye cream. Remember, there are no oil glands around the eyes, which is one reason why you get those pesky crow's feet. You need to dab plenty of eye cream around the area, never rubbing or pulling the skin, gently stippling with your fingertips." She demonstrated, gently rat-a-tat-tatting her index and middle fingers around her smile lines.

"Now, let's move on to exfoliation."

LUKE DIDN'T LIKE AUTOPSIES. He didn't like the industrial, disinfectant smells, the knives, the scales for weighing organs, the bone saw. He didn't like the casual way the medical examiners treated dead bodies or the fact that he should have conquered his nausea by now.

As always, he tried to concentrate on the facts Gil Sefton was throwing at him and Henderson.

"Death due to pericardial tamponade, secondary to a penetrating knife wound." He smiled at them. "Single knife wound killed her. Killer struck upward so the blade entered under the left breast and pierced the heart, causing blood to fill the sac around the heart—the pericardium—which then compressed the heart. She lost consciousness almost immediately and death occurred within two to five minutes."

"Time of death?" Henderson asked.

"Between ten-thirty and midnight."

"What can you tell us about the blade?" Luke asked.

"Six inches long. Straight across the top, comes to a sharp point, and curved on the bottom. Around a half inch, wider where it meets the handle. I'd say you're looking for something like a fishing knife." He pointed to a spot on the body. "See this mark here? Made by the hilt."

"She was killed in a hotel. Could the blade be some kind of chef's knife?"

Gil nodded. "A specialty carving knife of some sort. Sure. I'll have the full report to you guys tomorrow morning, but those are the highlights."

He turned to Henderson and said, "Let's check out the hotel kitchen, see if any of their knives are missing."

Henderson nodded. "And find out if the husband likes to fish." As they were leaving, Luke turned back. "Had she had sex recently?"

"Not that day."

"Thanks, Gil."

As they were heading out, Henderson's cell rang. He listened, seemed to tense slightly, then said, "Fine. Now is fine."

He turned to Luke. "It was the captain. He says the DA's office wants a quick update on the Neuman case and now would be good."

"They don't need both of us, Frank. You okay to take it? I'll check the hotel kitchen and then we'll go interview the husband."

LUKE APPRECIATED the smell of the hotel's kitchen a whole lot more than the morgue, but there were odd parallels between the two locations. A lot of stainless steel, tools of a trade he had no clue about, and people who made a career of cutting into dead things.

Lunch was over and dinner a few hours away, but still, the place was hopping. And the first person he bumped into didn't look like she cooked—not with diamond fingernails and a pale yellow sleeveless dress patterned with flowers.

"Toni."

"Detective, we'll have to stop meeting like this." She presented him with her slick, pearly smile, then, when she looked into his face, the smile faded and a tiny frown pulled her brows together. He thought he saw concern in her eyes. "Rough day?"

He was about to blow her off with some smart-ass remark, but instead, he nodded. "Yeah."

To his surprise, she touched his arm lightly. "I'm sorry."

"Goes with the job. What are you doing in the kitchen?"

"Checking on a special surprise dessert. It's Lady Bianca's birthday tomorrow. Even though she doesn't travel to the conference anymore, we thought it would be fun to arrange a huge cake for her and all sing; we'll do a live video feed. Of course, we have to eat cake pretty early in the day so she gets to see it before she goes to bed in England."

He knew that Lady Bianca was an American who bought herself a title and a fancy estate in England, but he hadn't realized she was still alive. "She must be pretty old."

She nodded. "Eighty. Which is a lot of candles." She grinned at him. "Luckily, it's a very big cake."

She opened her arms wide to illustrate and the way her biceps and triceps came to attention, he got the strong impression that Toni Diamond didn't spend all her time selling cosmetics. Some of it she spent working out.

"Who's in charge here?"

"Chef's over there. He's been a darling about the cake. " She turned and pointed, past a young guy with a huge bag of prawns in his hand, to a thin man with a mustache wearing a pristine apron and white hat who didn't look as though he partook of his own creations.

"Thanks."

"I'll introduce you."

"Not necessary," he said in a *Go Away* tone, but she tagged along anyway.

As he walked toward the head chef, the kitchen helper upended the bag and out spilled enough prawns, gray and curled, to coat half the ocean floor.

"Excuse me, Chef?" They made their way—him and his uninvited companion—over to the big stove where the chef was stirring something.

He glanced up, looked them up and down, took in the badge. "Help you?"

"I'm investigating the recent murder in the hotel a couple of nights ago. Any chance you're missing a knife?" It was like asking a lifeguard if the beach was missing a grain of sand. There were knives everywhere.

But the chef didn't laugh. He shook his head. "Can't tell about dinner knives or anything used out front. But the chefs are all maniacs about their knives. Believe me, if one was missing, I'd know."

"Okay. Thanks." He pulled out a card. "If you think of anything."

They turned, and the chef said, "There was one thing."

"What?"

"Lucy threw a fit a couple days ago, which is not unusual. Lucy gives PMS a bad name, if you know what I mean." Toni opened her mouth and Luke grabbed her wrist and squeezed it, hoping he could subtly communicate to her that feminist rants were better saved for after he'd finished work.

"What did she throw a fit about?"

"That's her coming out of the fridge. Go ask her."

Lucy was a muscular woman with a mass of curly black hair tied back. Her apron was stained, her cap on crooked and her face set in a frown. "Lucy?"

She glared at them, kicking the door to the walk-in fridge shut behind her. She glanced from Luke to Toni, and if possible, her frown deepened. "I already told you. The cake's under control. Got the perfect icing color match for the corporate logo, and yes, the specially ordered sparkly candles arrived." She tilted her hands like a cheerleader about to go into a routine. "All eighty of them. What do you want now? Sing along napkins?"

"Don't tempt her," he said, before Toni had a chance to speak. Then once more displayed his badge. "I'm a cop. Understand something happened with one of your knives?"

Her lip curled in a half grin. "You guys running out of crimes to solve?"

"It's in connection with the murder that happened here in the hotel."

"All my knives are here, but some cretinous moron put one of them in the dishwasher. Nobody touches my knives. I have to special order them from Japan."

"And you're sure the knife was yours?"

"Of course I'm sure," she snapped. "I mark all my knives." She stomped over to her station and pulled out a wicked-looking blade about six inches long and approximately half an inch wide. "See, here? I etch the blade with a special mark so I'd find them again if anybody stole them."

She glared at them both. "This isn't some junky Sunday roast carving knife your dad would use. My knives are the tools of my art. I wash them myself. By hand. Then some brainless millipede shoves this one in the dishwasher." Her voice rose to screeching heights.

"Did the culprit confess?"

She shook her head and set the knife down carefully. "Mood I was in, I'd have carved off his gonads and served them to him flambéed."

Luke took an involuntary half step back. "When did you discover the knife was in the dishwasher?"

Her forehead creased. She glanced at the knife and then at the two of them, comprehension dawning. "Oh, my God. You think that woman was killed with my knife?"

"We don't know anything yet, Lucy. We're making inquiries. When did you find the knife in the dishwasher?"

"Monday morning when I came on shift. Around eleven."

"I'm going to have to take your knife."

"Yeah. Sure." She looked at the thing as though she no longer wanted it anywhere near her. "I keep them sharp enough to..."

He got a fresh paper bag from the kitchen and bagged the knife.

Toni stayed with him as he left the kitchen. "Do you think that's the—"

"We don't know anything until it's tested."

She glanced at the bag then at him. "Was the murdered woman registered with the mystery conference? I heard she was."

"Your mother was right. You are nosy."

She sighed. "I know I am. But it seems so wrong for that young woman to be..."

"I know."

They stood for a moment, and he thought that behind the façade of cosmetics and the pushy personality, there was a woman of real character peeking out at him.

She gestured behind him. "Your partner's looking for you."

"Gotta go." Time to interview the husband. But before he went he pointed a finger at her. "And you keep your mouth shut about what happened in the kitchen."

"Of course."

"And stay out of trouble."

She gave him a half smile. "That I can't promise."

GREGORY NEUMAN WAS A SLOPPY DRUNK.

He answered the pounding on his hotel room door bleary-eyed and stinking. His nose was running, his fly was open and he had to hang on to the doorframe to remain upright. They should drag him around to AA meetings as an exhibit, Luke thought. He'd do a lot to turn drinkers off alcohol.

The guy pointed with a shaking finger to the Do Not Disturb sign lurching against the doorknob at the same approximate angle as the room's occupant.

"Mr. Neuman?"

He belched and belatedly stuck a polite hand in front of his mouth. "Sorry about the noise last night. It was only a chair. I'll pay for it." His eyes started to water. "My wife left me. Can you give me a break? Can you do that?"

Marciano and Henderson exchanged a glance. In his condition, nothing he said would be admissible in court. "May we come in?"

He was already staggering back to the bed, leaving the door wide open so they followed.

The place stank. Neuman stank.

He, or someone, had slept in both queen-sized beds and it was obvious housekeeping hadn't been in for a couple of days.

"Looks like you've been having quite the pity party," Henderson said, indicating the empties. Crumpled beer cans littered the floor along with a couple of empty wine bottles. An empty 26er of bourbon and another, half empty 26er sat on the vanity, a water glass about a third filled with booze beside it.

A chair that had obviously once matched the desk under the window lay on its side, one of the legs snapped. A navy Gore-Tex jacket sprawled on the floor—a garment more suited to Seattle rain than Texas heat—along with a pair of socks and a pair of sneakers. There was no suitcase in view. It seemed as though Neuman had followed his wife on impulse, not even taking time to pack. He looked and smelled like he'd been wearing and sleeping in the same clothes for a few days.

"Lost my wife," he mumbled, slumping on the bed and rubbing his hands over his face. His wedding ring shone in the light from the bedside lamp. No daylight entered the room since the drapes were drawn tight.

The ring was a typical man's gold wedding band. No way they'd have gone with this for him and a silver Celtic ring for the bride. Looked like she'd moved on and he hadn't.

"What do you mean, you lost your wife?"

"I told you. She's leaving me." He sniffed, rose from the bed and walked into the bathroom, Henderson closing in behind him, but his purpose was merely to grab a wad of toilet paper and wipe his nose and eyes. The tissue boxes were all empty.

He weaved his way back to the bed and collapsed. "Sorry about the mess." He scrubbed his hands over his eyes. "I don't know what to do."

"Why the fresh grief? She filed for divorce a month ago."

"Thought she changed her mind." He sniffled.

"What are you doing in Dallas, Mr. Neuman?"

"Came to see Amy. Tell her she was making a mistake." He eyed the water glass of bourbon. "Can I have a drink?"

Marciano crossed to the bathroom, rinsed out one of the used glasses he found in there and filled it with water. He came out and handed it to Gregory Neuman, who struggled to sitting then gulped water.

"What were you doing Sunday night?" Henderson asked.

"Sunday?" He rubbed his left temple as though trying to stimulate his brain. "I flew down to see my wife. She's here at a conference." He drank some water. "Got in around four. I called her but she didn't pick up. I left a couple messages."

He'd left four messages.

"I found out *he* was going to be here—"

"Who was going to be here?"

He turned to look from one of them to the other. "Why are you asking me all this? All I did was break a chair."

"Please, Mr. Neuman. If you could answer the question."

"Joseph Mandeville." He spat out the name.

He gulped more water. "She made him out to be some big deal but he was a two-bit user. Oh, and he likes the ladies. I was in Denver on business anyway so I decided to fly down here and beg her to come home with me." He shook his head. "But she didn't pick up."

"Then what happened?"

"She called me."

Henderson stopped scribbling and raised his head. "There's no record of that call on her cell phone log."

"Her battery was low. She called from the lobby phone of her hotel, I think."

"What time was that?"

"Maybe ten-thirty? Somethin' like that."

"What did she say?"

"She was coming over."

"Here? To this hotel?"

"Yeah. But she never showed up. I waited. For hours. Sat up all night." He shook his head. "I'm still waiting. She must have gone to him after all." He rubbed his wedding ring absently.

"When was the last time you saw your wife?"

"In Seattle. I don't know. Couple of weeks ago. Why?"

Luke took out the photograph. "Is this a picture of your wife?"

Neuman squinted at the photo. "What happened to her?"

"Is this Amy Neuman?"

"Yeah. That's my wife." His voice rose. "What the hell happened to her?"

"I'm sorry, Mr. Neuman. We've got bad news. Your wife's dead." He watched carefully to see how the man took the news, but with so much booze in his system he seemed to be having trouble comprehending.

"Dead?" He blinked. "She's thirty-five years old. She can't be dead."

"She was murdered."

"Oh, my God. No." And he burst into tears. "But she called me. I heard her voice."

"We're very sorry."

"No. You're wrong." He got off the bed, put the water down on the bedside table. "I'm gonna find her." Suddenly he put his hands to his head and bent over. "Why the hell did I drink so much? I can't think straight."

They didn't interrupt, merely let him talk.

"When? When did it happen?"

"Sunday night," Luke said.

"What were you doing Sunday night, Mr. Neuman?" Henderson asked.

He blinked as though the words hurt to hear. "You don't think I killed her. Why would I kill my own wife?" His voice went raspy. "I loved her."

"She was here to meet another man. She was leaving you."

"Not for him. He was stringing her along. Never had any serious inten...intent... Never had any serious plan. And now she's dead."

Tears spilled once more and, abandoning the wad of toilet paper, he grabbed a towel off the bed to wipe his eyes and blow his nose. "I should have walked over to meet her. Maybe if I had, she'd still be alive."

"Why didn't you?"

"She said she'd come here. Wanted to get out of the hotel. Didn't want to see him. She told me she was sorry."

He shook his head. "Why didn't I start walking? The marriage counselor told us to meet each other halfway."

The clock radio suddenly belted out a country and western tune, startling all of them. Neuman stared at it for a moment. Then he reached over and pushed the snooze button with an unsteady finger. "I'm supposed to catch a flight." He slumped back against the headboard, obviously realizing he wouldn't be going anywhere for a while.

"So your wife said she was coming over to meet you here, and she never showed up?" Henderson asked.

"Right. By yesterday I figured she'd changed her mind. I started drinking. And I got pretty mad and broke a chair. Thought Mandeville must have sweet-talked her back into his bed." He stared from one to the other of the detectives. "But he didn't. He killed her. You arrested him yet?"

"We have to ask you to identify the body."

He squeezed his eyes shut. "Okay. Let me shave first."

"Not now. Sober up. We'll come back for you in the morning. We'll take you in to identify your wife, and then we'll interview you again at the station. We need you sober, Mr. Neuman. Lay off the booze."

As Luke turned to leave, the last image he had of Gregory Neuman was of the man curled up in a ball, hugging one of the hotel pillows. He looked like a lost little kid hanging onto a stuffed animal.

"What do you think?" Henderson asked as they drove away.

"The sloppy drunk or the playboy author?" He shook his head. "I think Amy Neuman had bad taste in men. And that we should have another visit with our friend Mandeville."

CHAPTER 12

Men in general judge more from appearances than from reality. All men have eyes, but few have the gift of penetration.

–Niccoló Machiavelli

TONI HAD PICKED an early hour for her breakfast meeting, Wednesday morning, but even so there was a line up at the hotel's all-day restaurant. Tables were jammed together and those tables were packed with customers—most of them Lady Bianca reps snatching an early bite before the sessions or, like her, using this time during the conference to network with sales reps. Today she'd booked a breakfast meeting with Charlene Throckmorton, one of her newer reps.

Toni arrived first and the harried waitress plonked a stainless carafe of coffee on her table and a couple of menus, then rushed off.

It was soon apparent that Toni's appointment was running

late, which left her alone with her coffee at a table for two. Once upon a time, she'd have fidgeted and kept checking her watch, cursing the waste of time. Now she simply pulled her phone out of her bag and used the extra time to text message a reminder to all her reps. Tonight was the cutoff for orders that would qualify for the sales prizes.

"Check your stock, connect with your customers. Plan some make-over parties and get your orders in today. Let's win some bling!"

By the time she was done she had a cramp in her thumbs, but it was wonderful what attitude and clear goals could do for a person. If everyone in her division worked the phones and replenished their stock, they could still beat Nicole's group to some very nice diamonds. Still no sign of Charlene, so she pulled out the sales information on the new diamond hard eyebrow pencils and sent a second message to her reps reminding them of the revolutionary new product: *"Let's be original. How about an eyebrow party?! I'll take orders up until 11 p.m. Go girls!"*

She sipped her coffee and let the buzz of female chatter flow around her.

She knew an amazing number of the women currently eating breakfast, with the odd man dotted around. Orin Shellenbach was holding court with a few of the senior officers of the company, and in a quiet corner, she noted Thomas Feckler, enjoying a cozy breakfast with his wife. Normally, Melody and Nicole were inseparable so Toni was happy to see Melody had her husband around for balance.

The bustle of a couple leaving and another being seated at the table behind her barely ruffled her concentration until she heard the voice she'd know anywhere as Nicole Freedman's cut through her concentration like a buzz saw. Of all the tables in all the coffee shops...

Still, tiny annoyances are like raindrops, she reminded

herself, imagining a large lilac umbrella shielding her. She carried on for another couple of minutes doing her best to ignore Nicole and Stacy Krump, whose voice she also recognized.

Stacy had been with Lady Bianca less than a year and, as they all knew, the first year was critical. Within her first twelve months a woman either proved she had what it took to become a Lady Bianca star or it became clear there was no helium in her balloon. Toni liked to think she allowed her stars to rise naturally. Nicole was more of the push-them-until-they-break-out-or-give-up school of management.

"How's it going this month?" Nicole asked in her fake honey voice.

"Fine. Things are fantastic. I'm so happy to have this opportunity. Thank you for all your help."

"Well, I love you. I knew the second I saw you that you were someone special, the kind of woman who was born to greatness."

Oh, gag me.

"Thanks."

"How are you doing with your friendly fishing this month?" Friendly was the optimum attitude, but of course they were fishing for details about the woman so they'd know what bait might hook her in for an initial free facial and beauty consultation. Then they tried to recruit that woman as a customer, then a hostess to bring all her friends and family on board and then, if she seemed the right type, the consultant would talk the new hostess into becoming a Lady Bianca rep.

It was a brilliant strategy and had worked well enough that there were close to a million Lady Bianca reps in the world.

She could hear paper shuffling behind her and knew that Stacy had opened her progress binder. "I set myself a goal of approaching seventy-five strangers last month like we talked about. I went to every grocery store within thirty miles of my home and hung around two schools around quitting time. I thought that would be a good place to meet women with a few minutes to talk."

"That's fantastic. Shows great initiative," was the enthusiastic response.

"I only ended up talking to fifty-three women. And only forty-two of them would take my card."

"Okay, that's wonderful. You are really pushing beyond your comfort zone. I feel how exciting that is for you, even if it makes you a little nervous at first. And tell me you've booked consultations or parties with all forty-two of those women."

A soft giggle. "Hardly. I only got four phone numbers. Everybody else took my card and said they'd call me."

"You've got to get those phone numbers, honey. Women are so busy, they need for you to help them out by staying in touch and booking those appointments."

"I don't know how to make someone give me their number if they don't want to."

"I can help you with that. I've got some sales training material I can give you. I can even come with you next time and demonstrate. I am so proud of you." There was some rustling followed by smacking, smoochie noises, so Toni knew Nicole was in hug and kiss mode.

"Now, let's talk about this month's order. We need to get everything in before midnight tonight if we're going to win the division prize. I can really see a nice diamond ring on your finger. Right there." The top sales director in their division, which came down to either Nicole or Toni, stood to win the two-carat ring, but every one on their team would also win a modest diamond.

Toni could all but see Nicole reaching forward to playfully tap Stacy on her ring finger.

"I already put—"

Nicole interrupted. "How much new product do you need? I

personally over-ordered the new diamond hard eyebrow pencils. I'm sure we won't be able to keep them in stock. And with all those faces you're going to do next month, and the parties you'll hold, you're going to need to be ready. Remember, success rewards the prepared."

There was a pause. Even unable to see them, Toni could feel the weight of that silence. She'd stopped even the pretense of catching up on paperwork. She was eavesdropping with every cell of her body.

"The thing is, Larry is giving me a hard time about my credit card bills. He says I should be bringing in some money by now and not spending so much more than I'm making."

"Larry." It was said in the same tone one might mention *Bubonic Plague*.

"My husband?"

"Oh, I know who Larry is. And he's not the first husband who ever became jealous of his wife's success. Honey, would you open a jewelry store with one pair of earrings?"

"No."

"Of course you wouldn't. And you can't run a cosmetics business with no makeup. Inventory is essential to your success." Her voice dropped and Nicole could imagine her body language, leaning forward and cozying up to her prey. "You are on the road to success and riches beyond your wildest dreams. You've got the commitment, the drive, the talent, the team. All you have to do is keep believing in yourself and your future."

The clicking of crockery suggested that Stacy had taken refuge in her coffee mug. "But I still have to live with Larry. I can't handle another fight about money."

"It's really hard when you find out your partner isn't the supportive man you thought he was." There was a tiny pause. "I know. My former husband, Bill, never, ever supported me. But I got the last laugh. I live in a five thousand square foot chateau-style home with a swimming pool now. Bill lives with his mother."

"Are you suggesting I should divorce my husband?"

Sure sounded that way to Toni, who'd turned her head slightly to hear better. Encouraging women to get out there and hustle was part of the territory when you were a director, but browbeating them into buying more stock than they could afford was bad all around. Of course, Nicole received a commission on every product her sales reps purchased, and team prizes depended on the level of orders. With Toni and Nicole running neck-and-neck to winning the biggest prize in the region, they were both pushing for those extra orders. But to force a woman who clearly hadn't established her business yet into buying more than she felt comfortable with was, in the long run, bad business. Stacy would end up discouraged and quit, and Nicole would be short a rep.

"No, of course not, honey. I can't tell you whether your marriage is working for you anymore. Though plenty of women have gone on to be a lot more successful once they became single. Like me, for instance."

Not to mention that no human being could live with her.

"No. I'm going to suggest you separate your finances from your husband's."

"But we've always pooled our money. And he pays all the bills. He always has."

"Ready to order, ladies?" the waitress asked.

"I never eat breakfast," Nicole informed her. "Stacy?"

"Um, I'm not hungry."

"Just the bill, thank you."

"For two coffees," the woman said, with heavy sarcasm. "Right away."

"Your situation is exactly what I was afraid of. If you let Larry pay all your bills, then he's got control of you. You can't let that happen. You're an independent businesswoman now. You've got to stand up and accept your own success."

"But I haven't had any success," Stacy wailed.

"Of course you have. You approached forty-three women. You improved your friendly fishing skills. You'll set even more aggressive goals for next month and you'll meet them. I know you're going to make a lot of money. I feel it here, right in my heart. Embrace your best self!"

"But how would I do that?" She didn't sound too sure.

"Get your own credit card. I can help you apply for a company card. It's easy, and you'll both be a lot happier if Larry isn't too involved in your business. Later, when you've got a large bank balance, you can surprise him. Most men come around when they see our happiness—and the new car parked in the new driveway."

"I could get my own credit card?"

"Absolutely. We can get that done today, then you'll be able to put in the kind of order that shows you are ready to go to the next level."

"I don't know, what if—"

"People want to be associated with winners, Stacy. That means you have to act like a winner. Positive attitude will bring positive results."

"But Larry—"

"Is this your business or a little hobby on the side?" Nicole asked sharply.

"It's a business, of course." But Stacy sounded more nervous of Nicole than sure of her prospects for success.

"Then you've got to invest in yourself. Do you think Bill Gates or Steve Jobs—God rest his soul—worried about how much money they were spending on electronic parts when they started their businesses in their parents' garages?"

"No, but—"

"Think about that every time you log onto your computer.

And where would we be if Lady Bianca had stopped experimenting with cosmetics in her kitchen, given up and gone on welfare?"

"Well, we'd be—"

"We'd be nowhere. That's where. We wouldn't be having this conversation because there wouldn't be a billion-dollar Lady Bianca empire, and you wouldn't be part of the top-selling team in our division. For the third year in a row."

This was too much for Toni. She'd sat quiet as long as she could. She turned, caught the fleeting look of annoyance on Nicole's face and let them both bask in the warmth of her smile. "You're not quite there yet, Nicole. The end of year results won't be tallied until tomorrow. Last time I looked our unit and your unit were so close in sales volume it's still anybody's game."

Nicole's trilling laugh split her lips open like a hatchet to reveal teeth so perfect they could have come out of a Tiffany's box. "Positive thinking, darling. See the vision, believe in the vision, achieve the vision."

"Oh, our team believes in positive thinking too. In fact, I'm positive this time we'll beat you in sales volume." She turned to Stacy. "A little friendly rivalry is always good, you know. Keeps us on our toes."

Nicole rose, probably so she could look down on Toni. "Looks like you were stood up for breakfast. Hope it wasn't somebody on your team."

Stacy also rose. Two bright spots burned on her cheeks and she'd worn all her lipstick off, probably from nerves. "I better go. I've got to get to my first session."

"Of course," Nicole said warmly. "Find me at lunch. We'll get you signed up for your new card right after we eat."

"Okay. Thanks for everything." After a quick hug, Stacy left, her Lady Bianca conference bag swinging from her arm.

Nicole made to follow her. Toni tried to let the woman go,

reminding herself that Stacy's affairs were none of her business but, as usual, she couldn't stop herself from butting in.

"Nicole, do you have a minute? Let me buy you a cup of coffee."

"All right. I'll move to join you. Your table is still so nice and fresh."

She moved over and sat down. "Look, don't take what I said there too seriously. You know how it is. We have to keep the troops motivated. Your team has as good a chance of finishing first as mine does, but a little healthy competition never hurt anyone, right?"

"Absolutely. I'm not worried about that." She felt her face begin to crease in a frown, pictured Botox needles and smoothed out her forehead. "I wonder if you should encourage Stacy to apply for another credit card if she's already taking flak at home from her husband. I know it's none of my business, but as an impartial observer I saw how uncomfortable she was at the thought of more debt. Sometimes these girls have to build confidence by selling more of the stock they have before ordering more."

Nicole made a show of examining her flawless manicure. She had beautiful hands, with long tapered fingers and, as both of them knew, the two biggest rings that sparkled on them were for heading the top-selling team for the last two years. "I know you're jealous of my success," she finally said, still looking at her hands. "But I wouldn't have believed you'd stoop so low as to sabotage me and my recruits."

Toni should have kept her nose out of Stacy's affairs. She'd known it. Nicole was never going to listen to her or see reason. She was the kind of sales director who got lambasted on Internet websites.

"I'm only suggesting that maybe Stacy would be happier if she spent more time selling her current product and held a few more skincare and makeup classes to build her customer base before she orders a lot more product."

"Those orders will earn me another diamond ring and keep your fingers empty," Nicole snapped. With that, she stood so abruptly that the waitress nearly spilled the fresh pot of coffee she was carrying down the front of her uniform.

Nicole glared at them both. "Have a nice day."

CHAPTER 13

Mirrors should think longer before they reflect.

–Jean Cocteau

CHARLENE THROCKMORTON ARRIVED SLIGHTLY out of breath to her breakfast meeting. "I'm so sorry, Toni. I slept in."

"It's obvious to everyone you slept in. Your hair's all over the place, you slapped that makeup on in record time and your skirt is around the wrong way."

"Oh, geez." The girl giggled nervously and spun the skirt on her skinny waist. "There. Sorry. I haven't been sleeping well." She dropped her voice. "That murder kind of freaked me out being right here in the hotel and all."

"All right. No point fretting about a tragedy that's nothing to do with us." She relented. The murder was on her mind, too. "Luckily for you I'm not a client or I might not have waited. Now, have some coffee and let's order breakfast. We can eat while we talk."

They made small talk until their breakfast was before them. Charlene was a bright, pretty flight attendant who was trying to build a second income so she could stay home and have a baby. She was big on enthusiasm but Toni was beginning to suspect she wasn't great at follow-through.

They both ordered yogurt and fruit and when it was before them, Toni said, "All right. Tell me about your goals for the next year."

"Well, I want to sell a lot more product, and I'm going to recruit some more girls onto my team and of course, I want to make more money."

"That's wonderful. Those are fun daydreams, aren't they?"

Charlene nodded but she looked a little wary. As well she should. Had she not read any of the training material?

"Goals are quantifiable, Charlene. For instance, book and hold ten facial home parties next month. Friendly Fish fifty people by the end of the month. Daily, weekly, monthly, yearly, you have to be able to say, how much will I accomplish and by when? Then it's measurable." She stopped to sip her ice water. She felt like she was regurgitating the same words she'd repeated in exactly that way a thousand times before. Probably because she had.

"Success starts with positive thinking, conceive it so you can achieve it. But then you have to get out there and do the work."

"I know my goal is to stay home and have a family," Charlene said, sounding a little like the kid who got called out for not doing her homework.

"Then let's make it possible. Now, take out your training binder and let's set you some concrete, achievable goals. And then I want you to get out there and have a great conference."

Her phone was making the chirping sound it made when she had received a text message. It was from Tiffany.

. . .

Hey Mom, I replaced all Grandma's country CDs with some sick tunes!

She texted back.

What did you replace them with???

The answer came back so fast she knew her daughter had been waiting to hear from her.

Metallica, Iron Maiden, Rammstein. Looking for Nirvana rt now.

She smiled, sitting there in the coffee shop. It was her daughter's way of saying, *I miss you*. Of course, Tiffany would never replace her grandmother's beloved Dolly Parton CDs with heavy metal. Toni was thirty-five percent sure.

She got busy with her thumbs once more.

Miss you. Be good!

"What do you think?" Henderson asked Marciano as they sat at their desks, with their chairs swiveled so they could see each other. Luke drank bad office-brewed coffee, Henderson sipped green tea he brought from home in a thermos. "You think Neuman killed his wife?"

"Not after I watched him ID her this morning. He was a truly broken man. Then he puked."

"With his hangover, you'd have puked too."

"That smell in there is enough to make anybody sick."

"His story was the same when he was drunk as it was when he was sober. He didn't hesitate about voluntary consent to a search of his hotel room and belongings. But he had motive, opportunity. He calls her four times and next thing she's dead."

Luke gulped more coffee. As though it might help clear his mind. "My money's on Mandeville."

"We've got no evidence. Nothing to hold him." Henderson sipped his tea. "He lied to us about the fight. Stupid thing to do when he must have known we'd check out the restaurant."

"Maybe he hoped nobody would remember them."

"So, he also had means, he had opportunity. But where's the motive?"

"Because he could. His book's got a section about using what's at hand to do the deed. Like a knife out of the hotel kitchen."

"Pretty weak."

"Yeah. Did the husband do it to stop her going to the boyfriend? Did the boyfriend do it to stop her going back to the husband? Or because he wanted a new chapter for his next book? It feels like we're missing something the size of an asteroid."

"Maybe the knife will turn up something."

"Yeah. I put a rush on it, so if we're lucky we'll get DNA results by Monday. I'm going to get caught up on the paperwork." Keeping up what they termed the murder book was an important part of the investigation. So far it contained photographs, transcripts of interviews, and the initial crime scene report. By the time the case went to trial, there would be thousands of pages of documents and hours of video.

He opened the binder and gazed down at the first picture of Amy, taken at the scene. "Who killed you?" he asked silently. "And why?"

STACY KRUMP WAS STANDING outside the conference meeting room Toni was about to enter for the session titled: Creative Marketing Strategies Using Social Media. It was such an uncreative title she had doubts about the workshop.

"Hi, Stacy," she said, preparing to go around the woman standing there like a stone statue.

The sessions were changing over so there was plenty of coming and going, women chattering, giggling and hugging.

There was always plenty of hugging going on at a Lady Bianca convention, and right now Stacy looked as though she needed one badly.

"Stacy, is everything all right?"

She started and blushed. "Oh, Toni. I—" She glanced nervously behind Toni's shoulder, no doubt terrified Nicole would see them together and she'd get in trouble.

Toni knew it was partly her fault poor Stacy was acting this way, so she pulled herself up to her full height, as she always did when called upon to do something unpleasant and said, "I need to apologize to you about this morning. I was out of line. I never should have interrupted you and Nicole."

"Oh, well, that's okay. You were there. You heard her say I should get a company credit card and she'd help me. So then I wouldn't have to let my husband know about my finances."

"Yes. And it's a personal decision. If you think that would be good for your business, you should go ahead and get one, but there's nothing wrong with thinking it over for a night or two."

Stacy rubbed her conference agenda between her fingers leaving a damp mark. "Well," she giggled nervously, "the thing is I already have a card." She glanced up and back down at the agenda. "I got one today."

"Oh." Toni didn't know what else to say.

"Nicole helped me. And then we did some shopping." She was rubbing the agenda faster and faster, soon the paper would tear. Then, in a rush she blurted, "I put five thousand dollars on that card."

And she burst out crying.

Now, Toni had been with Lady Bianca for more than fifteen years and she'd been cried on a time or two, so she took the gush of tears in her stride.

"Come on," she said, "let's get away from this crowd and find somewhere to sit down. Then I'll get you some water."

"I didn't mean to spend that much, but it seemed like it was the best thing to do and I'll make twice that back when I sell all the product." She hiccupped. "But I'm not real good at selling yet. And if my husband finds out, he'll—"

"Toni!" Nicole's angry voice cut through the giggling, chatting and hugging crowd like machine gun fire. "What are you doing making one of my girls cry?"

She grabbed Stacy's shoulders and physically yanked her away from Toni.

Women around them stopped and stunned silence surrounded them.

Toni had a temper and unfortunately, when it flared it tended to run hot and rash. Right now she was so angry with Nicole that even if the woman had acted as angelic as the Virgin Mary she'd have wanted to smack her.

"Me?" she shouted back. "I didn't make this poor woman cry. You did. You forced a credit card on her she doesn't want or need and put a big balance on it. Why? So you can win yourself another diamond ring. That's cheap, Nicole. It's cheap and sleazy."

"Get off your high horse. That order alone will be enough to make sure we beat you again this year." Nicole rubbed Stacy's arm in what was probably supposed to be a soothing gesture, but she was so mad her arm jerked up and down, looking like a dog humping a chair leg.

"You should be so proud, Stacy. Your order got us to the top. For the third year in a row."

"That's going to be cold comfort when she can't pay the bills she's racked up. Why aren't you helping her sell what she already has?"

"If you weren't spying on us at breakfast you wouldn't know anything about Stacy's business. It's private."

The object of the fight was alternating between bright red blushes and pale shades. "Please. Stop shouting," Stacy pleaded. "I'm getting a migraine."

But the two were in it now and this fight had been brewing for a decade. One little migraine wasn't going to stop them.

"Spying?" The word shrieked out, with Toni hitting a high note she hadn't known was in her vocal range. "I would never stoop to spy on you. I overheard you encouraging Stacy to get a divorce."

Nicole shoved herself right into Toni's personal space and jabbed her in the chest with a talon-like fingernail. "Keep your big nose out of my business. Or you'll be sorry."

"Are you threatening me?"

Nicole jumped back so fast she landed on Stacy's instep, causing the younger woman to howl. But her eyes stayed on Toni's, hard and bright. For a second there was absolute silence. Toni could see her thin chest rising up and down like she was panting. Finally she pointed and said, "My God. It's you," in the same voice Macbeth uses when he sees Banquo's ghost.

"Me what? What are you talking about?"

"You've been sending me those notes." Her breath huffed in and out.

Nicole was staring at her with such hatred in her eyes that Toni felt physically stung by it. She had no idea what the woman was raving about.

"What notes?"

She glanced around and her gaze landed on Melody Feckler, who looked as though she'd been slapped with a dead fish.

Toni knew exactly how she felt.

The silence was as thick as the morning the dead woman was found. She heard her own harsh breathing and that of Nicole's.

"I always knew you were jealous of me, but now I see that you truly hate me."

"Nicole, I don't have a clue what you're talking about."

Her hand was shaking when she pointed at Toni. "I'll stop you, you witch."

CHAPTER 14

If I were two faced, would I be wearing this one?

–Antonio Machado

Toni crept in late to *Creative Marketing Strategies Using Social Media* and then couldn't concentrate anyway. She could imagine herself and Nicole as the subject of a lot of tweets and Facebook updates. She was furious with Nicole. But in her deepest self she was ashamed that she'd let herself stoop to her rival's level. She cut out of the rest of the afternoon sessions and spent an hour in the hotel gym working off her frustrations, followed by a twenty-minute soothing face mask during which she listened to a motivational podcast.

She picked up her phone and called Tiff and was grateful when her daughter actually answered. "Hi, hon, how's it going?"

"Good. Grandma's rocking out to Iron Maiden."

She chuckled, feeling better already. "I bet. And what did you do today?"

"Not much. Smoked some crack. Got a tattoo. Joined the Hell's Angels. Pretty quiet day."

"Don't forget your bike helmet."

Tiffany snorted. "You are such a mom."

There was a short pause. "How 'bout you?" her daughter asked. "What did you do?"

"Not much. Got into a public brawl. Had a cat fight with another rep."

"Yeah, right."

If only she were joking. "Are you eating all right?"

"Sure. I explained the low-calorie aspects of veganism to Grandma and now she's totally into it. I think she's becoming a vegan too."

"You'd better join Lady Bianca, Tiff. You were born to sell."

By the time she'd showered and re-done her makeup, going a little heavier than usual and putting extra shimmer on her cheeks, almost in defiance, she felt a lot better.

Still, it was a somber group of her reps who met for dinner.

The lobby sported a marble statue of a horse, a landmark that made a good meeting spot to gather a group together to go out for a meal. Unfortunately, Nicole had chosen the same meeting spot. Naturally, she and Toni ignored each other. Where she'd slapped on extra make-up, Nicole had splashed out on her outfit. She wore a cream silk wrap dress and shoes that smote Toni with envy. They were cream and made of fine leather, sporting gold bows on the sides.

"If she paints a stripe of White-out across the front of her hair, she's all set to be Cruella de Vil at Halloween," Suzanne Mireille said into Toni's ear, in her husky French-accented voice.

Toni chuckled, "Well, God love her. Somebody's got to."

Then turned to her friend and sales rep. "You heard about the fight?"

The shrug was pure Gallic. "Who didn't? She's not worth your time."

"They've won, though. You know that. Stacy's five grand makes them uncatchable now. I'm taking orders until eleven, but there's no way I'll get that kind of commitment in the next couple of hours."

"So, we'll win next year. Trust me, we all want to bring that nasty woman down," Suzanne said. In various ways, all of Toni's team echoed those sentiments, but it was still a quiet group dinner.

Orin Shellenbach approached her when she returned from dinner with her sales team. "Toni, I'm so glad I caught you," he said with his usual Hollywood gushiness, as though about to tell her that she'd won the side-by-side refrigerator *and* the self-cleaning oven. "Let me buy you a drink."

She was tired, overwrought, and knowing they'd lost the top sales spot to Nicole's group had put a pall over dinner. She didn't want to get her hand slapped for fighting in public, even if she did deserve it. But she knew Orin was only doing his job, and she figured she might as well get the lecture over with. She put her own fake smile on and said to the group, "I'll see you all in the morning."

Suzanne looked as though she was going to say something, but thought better of it. She touched Toni's shoulder in silent support and headed off with the rest of the girls.

"Let's go out of the hotel. It's so crowded in the bar here."

For that, she was grateful. At least he wasn't going to dress her down in a bar full of curious women. He led her to a Starbucks attached to the mall across the street, which fortunately contained no Lady Bianca reps.

She waited until he'd brought her an iced tea and was sitting across from her at a round table by the window.

She took a long, cold drink, then said, "I guess you heard what happened today."

"I'm glad you brought that up, Toni. You created quite a sensation. I had Nicole almost in hysterics and, as you can imagine, there's a lot of gossip. You know that as directors, you have to set an example for other reps."

Typical that the woman had gone running to daddy to tell on Toni, as though she hadn't behaved equally badly. "Nicole certainly seemed recovered enough from her hysterics to go for dinner with her team. And to gloat about getting the top sales spot. Again."

He rubbed a thumb along his tanned jaw. Rumor was that he'd purchased his own tanning bed and used it every day. "She says you're so jealous you're trying to destroy her credibility."

Toni took a long sip of tea. Cold. Tart. Made herself take a full breath before she answered. "I regret losing my temper with her in public. But, Orin, she's pushing her sales reps to buy more stock than they're comfortable with. One of her reps was in tears over it. That's not how Lady Bianca works."

"None of her reps are complaining, Toni. They love her."

"They're brainwashed."

He sipped his own tea and then said, "This isn't sour grapes because she beat you, is it?"

"No. But I resent that she forced that poor woman to buy five thousand dollars worth of extra merchandise so they could win."

"It wasn't only that. Another of Nicole's reps placed an order for ten thousand."

She felt her eyes bug out. "Ten thousand dollars? A single rep? She'd have to sell twenty grand this month. That's ludicrous."

"It shows confidence in her sales ability that you have to admire. All your reps combined only brought in another four thousand today. Unless you get another eleven thousand in the next hour or so, she won fair and square."

"Who put in a ten thousand dollar order?"

He looked at her from under his eyebrows. The posture put his chin closer to the crisp white shirt he wore to emphasize his tan. The reflection made her glad her foundation was SPF 15.

"You know I can't tell you that."

She looked out the window and across the highway. The hotel rose up in the night sky, ablaze with lights. Her girls had worked so hard. It wasn't fair.

"We both lost our tempers," she conceded. "It won't happen again."

He put his joined hands underneath his chin as though he were about to pray. His blue eyes grew solemn. "Nicole also tells me you've been threatening her."

Now this was going too far. "She was the one who threatened me, Orin. And hundreds of reps heard her."

"No. Not today. She says you've been sending her threatening emails."

"Then she's lying." Toni always tried to be fair, so she added, "Or crazy."

"I told her it didn't sound like something you'd do." High praise indeed. "But she insists she's been getting them for months."

"They why didn't she call me on it before now?"

"They are anonymous."

"If they're anonymous, why does she think they're from me?" When he didn't answer, she shook her head. "I'm a pretty direct person. If I have a problem with someone, I let them know it." She tapped her fingernails against the tabletop. "Where are these emails?"

"I think she destroyed them. She wouldn't want to keep negative energy in her work space."

"Well, then she'd better Feng Shui her threats against me

out of her space, too. I didn't send her any threatening emails. Believe me."

"Good. Look, I like you and Nicole but you have to learn to co-exist."

"We will. I'll do everything in my power to avoid her. And when I see her I'll pretend she's invisible."

"Toni—"

"It's the best I can promise."

At that moment the door opened and a quartet of Lady Bianca women entered. They saw Orin and eight eyes went wide. He was a celebrity of sorts at the convention, being so senior in the company and a man. Good looking even, if you liked the game show host type. He seemed to enjoy his position and usually spent as much time as he could rallying the troops.

"I'm going to head back now, Orin. Thanks for the tea."

"Do you want me to walk back over with you?"

"No, thanks. Now that it's cooler, I think I'll take a walk. See you tomorrow." And maybe the exercise and fresh air would help her temper simmer down.

As she opened the door to leave she heard Orin behind her saying, "And how are you lovely ladies tonight?"

A LONG, brisk walk through the hotel grounds and down a couple of side streets and back again calmed Toni enough that she could return to the hotel and hopefully get a good night's sleep. Tomorrow, she was sure she'd have her equilibrium back. And one day, she'd probably laugh about that ridiculous fight.

It was late but she wasn't tired. Maybe she'd watch a movie on TV to relax. Normally when she couldn't sleep she worked on her business, but tonight she couldn't summon the enthusiasm.

Toni's steps echoed as she made her way across the deserted lobby heading for her room. It was funny being so alone when the place was crowded all day. She knew there were thousands of people in the building, but none were visible. Probably a few were still in the bar, but she had no interest in checking.

The elevators yawned, silver escalator steps slid up and down empty. The coffee bar that had been hopping all day was dark and shrouded. Her heels made so much noise on the marble floor they sounded like tap shoes.

She, however, did not feel like dancing.

She was mad. Mad at Nicole for putting her in this position, mad at Orin for calling her on her bad behavior but most of all mad at herself for snapping earlier today.

As she walked she realized she'd had too much iced tea and the liquid made its presence felt. She could wait until she reached her room but she had a morbid fear of getting stuck in an elevator and having to pee.

She detoured into the conference level washroom where so much primping, gossiping, and consoling went on during the day. It was oddly silent at this time of night and without all the women in there it seemed awfully big—a huge marble tomb.

Oh, no, not empty, she realized, seeing a pair of shoes under the door of one stall. Definitely a Lady Bianca rep, though, if the cream pumps were any indication. Then she recognized the gold bow ornament on the side of the shoes and knew they didn't belong to any old Lady Bianca rep. Unless Payless was running a sale on cream pumps with a bow buckle—and somehow she doubted those shoes came from any discount store, she'd managed to get some alone time with the only person in the entire organization she really truly loathed.

Nicole Freedman.

Toni delicately chose a stall far from Nicole's. Did her thing and came out. While she was washing her hands she studied her reflection in the mirror and was horrified at how dry her lips looked. Facing Nicole one on one at almost midnight was bad enough, but she would not do it with dry, cracking lips. When she got upstairs she'd exfoliate them with a package of the hotel's sugar and a little of the almond oil she never traveled without. A little sugar mixed with the oil scrubbed on the lips and they'd be free of the roughness. A few days of extra lip balm and her lips would be as dewy and fresh as new berries.

She unzipped her bag and dug out a restorative lip gloss that contained aloe, vitamin E and beeswax all in a pale raspberry tone with just a hint of sparkle. She swiped the product over her lips, straightened her jacket and turned when an odd feeling like a draft from an open window gave her goose bumps.

Nicole's stall had been quiet and still for a while.

The shoes were the right color and had the bows but Toni couldn't imagine Nicole, even on the toilet, letting her legs sprawl like that.

None of her business if Nicole was having a problem. She took a step away then found she couldn't leave without making sure whoever was in there was okay.

"Nicole?" she called softly. "Is that you?"

There was no answer.

"Nicole?" A little louder this time.

Nothing.

"I know you're angry with me, but I wish you'd answer me. Then I can leave."

This was ridiculous and undignified. She raised her gaze to the shiny tiled ceiling. "Nicole? Do you need some help?"

Nothing. Utter silence. Maybe it wasn't Nicole.

"Whoever is in the bathroom, are you all right?"

Still nothing. Toni did not want to intrude if the woman was having a crying jag or something and desperate to be left alone, but she couldn't shake the feeling that something was amiss. She stepped closer to the stall and noticed that the door wasn't latched shut.

The hairs on the back of her neck rose as she walked forward, hearing her heels clack on the tile floor.

For some strange reason, she whispered. "Are you okay?"

She was in front of the door. There was maybe half an inch of space gaping where it wasn't fully closed. She swallowed. "I'm coming in. Stop me if you don't want me to."

No response.

She pushed the door open. And then wished she hadn't.

It was Nicole. Or, more accurately, what was left of Nicole. She was in the same outfit she'd been wearing earlier. The gorgeous cream dress.

Nicole's head was back and her eyes were open so it looked as though she were counting ceiling tiles.

But she wasn't counting ceiling tiles.

There was a blood-soaked hole in her chest and protruding from it was the black handle of a knife. "Oh, no."

Not again.

CHAPTER 15

Every man at the bottom of his heart believes that he is a born detective.

–John Buchan

TONI DISCOVERED two things while she was standing there. One: reading about a person discovering a dead body or watching it on television is very different from actually doing it. Two: she was not as brave as she thought.

She knew she had to find out whether Nicole was still alive, which meant she had to touch the woman. Toni thought the chances that there was life in that body were slim, given the wound and the amount of blood that soaked the cream silk, but obviously, it was important to be sure. Imagine if she could have saved Nicole's life and didn't because she was too scared.

For a second, Toni thought she heard Nicole breathing, then realized she was wheezing loud enough for both of them. Reaching forward, Toni felt under Nicole's ear and down her neck, trying to locate the same pulse point she monitored on herself while exercising. She discovered it's not easy to find another person's pulse, especially when your own is banging away inside your head like the entire cast of Stomp on speed.

She felt around a bit, pushing her middle and ring fingers into flesh that was cool and rubbery, but she didn't feel anything. She kept her eyes turned away from that awful knife hilt on the left side of her chest. Around where her heart must be. Toni reached for her cell phone and backed away.

She bumped into something. She would have screamed, but terror clogged her throat. She spun around only to see that the door had shut behind her. In her panic, Toni dropped her cell phone, which sounded like an explosion as the metal device hit the floor tile, then slid under the stall and into the next one. She bolted out of Nicole's stall and dove to the floor to retrieve her phone.

She called 9-1-1. Her hands were shaking so badly she had to punch the numbers in three times before she got it right.

She knew she should stay until the police arrived, so she paced the bathroom floor a few times, telling herself to calm down. She didn't want to look but as she paced Nicole's legs kept coming into her range of vision under the stall, like the Wicked Witch of the West's after Dorothy's house falls on her and all you can see is her lower legs and her shoes.

Then Toni did the oddest thing, which ever afterward she would associate with shock. She went back to the stall and pushed Nicole's knees and ankles together and neatened up her skirt. It was crazy, interfering with a body like that, but she couldn't stop herself. If she had an enemy in the world it was Nicole, but she thought of how much her appearance mattered to her and how mortified she'd be to have strangers seeing her sprawled out like that.

Toni couldn't bring her back to life, but at least she could ensure she was sitting modestly when the police arrived.

Maybe doing this one kindness after death would help balance the negative things she'd thought about the woman in life.

Nicole hadn't started to stiffen yet. And there was no stubble on her legs, Toni noticed when she smoothed her skirt. She rose, her stomach rebelling against the smell. She'd have thought a murder scene would smell like a butcher's shop, but it didn't. God help her, the blood smell was fresher and she caught a hint of metal in the air.

As Toni backed away to wash her hands yet again she realized that Nicole, who was as fastidious as Toni about her appearance, wasn't wearing her pantyhose.

It was so quiet in that bathroom. Toni was scared to walk out of there and scared to remain. What if Nicole's killer came back?

She wanted very badly to run up to her room. Sprint in fact, then burrow into the bedclothes and stick a pillow over her head. Logic told her the killer was not going to come back to the bathroom, but logic didn't stop her heart from banging or her hands from shaking. However, she found she couldn't leave Nicole. Maybe it was guilt from their fight that afternoon, but she felt oddly protective.

Luckily, she didn't have to stand guard for long, nor did the killer return. Around seven minutes after she placed the call the first uniformed officers arrived. Once the cops were on scene, Toni started to breathe normally again.

The first officers confirmed Toni's identity as the person who'd called in the death, and then did pretty much what she had done. They checked Nicole's pulse and confirmed she was dead.

"I'll call the street sergeant," the first cop said to the second. They'd introduced themselves but she couldn't remember their names. Her head felt fuzzy.

The second officer walked up to Toni. "We need to secure the area. You'll have to wait outside."

She nodded.

"But stay close. Somebody will want to interview you."

"Of course."

She sat in an area of comfy chairs near the elevators. She was aware of activity in and around the bathroom but she'd lost interest. She wrapped her arms around herself. The air conditioning seemed to be on overdrive and she was shivering.

A little while later, four more uniforms headed off, all in different directions of the hotel, presumably looking for a guy with blood all over him and a guilty expression on his face. She hoped they found the killer fast.

Nobody seemed too bothered about Toni, so she stayed out of the way and waited. The same white-haired coroner who'd taken away the first murder victim walked past. The thought flitted through her mind that he was having a busy week.

For once it didn't even occur to her to make use of the extra minutes by pulling some activity out of her bag. Instead, she sat there and let her mind wander. Unfortunately, her mind didn't want to go anywhere happy. It insisted on revisiting that last time she and Nicole had been together when they'd both uttered words they were bound to regret.

While she waited, a tall, gray-haired man whose eyelids drooped with fatigue came toward her carrying a tray. He wore a gray suit with a rectangular gold name badge that all the hotel staff wore.

"Excuse me. I'm Armand Santiago, the hotel manager," he said to her. "I am devastated that you should have suffered such a shock. I've brought you some hot tea."

"Thank you."

He set the tray down. "I can't believe such a thing has happened." He didn't add *again*, but the word rattled in the silence. His voice was smooth and soothing, as she supposed the manager of a large hotel's would be, but he couldn't keep the worry out of his tone. Two murders in a week could not be good for business.

She was surprised at how badly her hands were still shaking as she reached for the pot.

Without any indication that he'd noticed her distress, Armand Santiago said, "May I?" and reached for the pot.

She nodded gratefully.

"Cream and sugar? Or lemon?"

"Lemon. Thank you." He poured a stream of some kind of scented tea into her cup. She didn't care what it was or whether it contained caffeine. Somehow, she didn't think she'd sleep much tonight. Using silver tongs he expertly popped a wedge of fresh lemon into her cup and handed it to her.

She sipped the hot tea and wrapped her hands around the white china, letting the warmth seep into her.

"Is there anything else I can get you?"

"No. Thank you. The tea is wonderful."

He nodded. "I'll be in my office if you need me for anything." Then, with a worried glance at the bathroom, he walked briskly away.

As the person who had discovered the body, Toni knew someone was going to want to talk to her sometime.

She was right both in that somebody would want to talk to her and in her guess as to who it would be. Luke and his partner appeared together. Detective Henderson had had his cut re-buzzed since she'd last seen him. Luke touched her arm and gave it a reassuring squeeze. "You okay?"

She nodded. It was a lie, of course, but she didn't think freaking out was going to help anybody.

When she turned her head she saw that the CSI people were back. She wondered how much useful forensic evidence a person could find in a public washroom. No doubt somebody attending the mystery readers' conference would know.

She was getting tired. It was after one in the morning and the adrenaline that had kept her going was ebbing.

Two pairs of eyes stared at her. Warm, deep brown and cool glacier blue/gray.

"Toni, we'd like you to come down to the station with us."

She was so startled she sipped too much tea and burned her tongue. "The station?"

"We'd like to ask you some questions and tape the interview."

"Oh. Okay."

She took a last sip of her tea and set the cup down. They didn't talk as they walked through the lobby. She glanced at the car park elevator. "Should I take my own car?"

Luke shook his head. "We'll give you a ride back."

"Okay."

There were a number of police vehicles out front, lights flashing. She saw a TV news van already unloading equipment and was happy to be hustled to an unobtrusive, unmarked dark blue Taurus. She got into the back. Henderson drove.

When they arrived at police headquarters, which was situated in Corvallis City Hall, she got out of the car, wishing she'd chosen something less spicy for dinner than the chicken enchilada platter. Her stomach felt jumpy.

They led her inside and up an elevator to the fourth floor. A uniformed guy behind a glass wall nodded to Luke. "Hey, Sarge."

They led her to a door marked *Interview Room*.

"The camera and microphone activate automatically when I open the door," he informed her.

She nodded. "Ready."

The room was around eight feet square, with no furniture but a rectangular table and four chairs and two wall-mounted cameras. Luke and his partner indicated where she should sit

—facing the cameras, while they seated themselves across from her.

The sounds of chairs scraping linoleum and the quiet thump of her bag as she set it down were the only sounds she could hear.

Luke sent her a reassuring smile. Then glanced at his watch. "It's one-seventeen a.m. August first. I'm Detective Sergeant Luke Marciano. With me is Detective Sergeant Frank Henderson and Ms. Toni Diamond, regarding the incidents that took place earlier today."

Once more he looked at her. "Tell me about your evening?"

Such an innocuous question, the kind her mother might ask her after a date with a new man. No, more neutral in tone. More the way she'd ask her own daughter how she'd spent the evening, careful to let no sense of wild curiosity sneak into her tone. The trouble with a secretive child was that they so easily shut down completely in the information department. Tiffany kept all her sharing and chattering for Facebook and texting her friends.

And now Tiff was going to have to deal with the fact that her mother was involved in another murder.

"My evening. Let's see." Her mind felt strangely blank. Recalling her evening was like trying to dredge up the details of her summer holiday and now she couldn't even remember where she'd gone. Or trying to remember who won all the categories of last year's Oscars. She had been rehearsing the story of *How She Discovered Nicole Dead in the Bathroom* and now it seemed they wanted something else from her. Or at least, a prequel.

But she took one look at his serious face and knew that recalling all the details she could was more important than who won best supporting actress last year.

And then it all came back.

"I was with my Lady Bianca sales team. We all had dinner together at a Mexican restaurant in the Old Town."

He nodded. Was there a glimmer of relief in his gaze? She hoped so. She paused but no one said anything. She'd sort of expected a Q&A but it seemed they just wanted her to ramble.

"Um. Let me think. We met in the lobby of the Weymouth Hotel at seven. We didn't leave until seven-twelve or so because Charlene Throckmorton was late, as usual." She suddenly realized that no one in the police department knew or cared about Charlene Throckmorton. She needed to get a grip.

"We got to the restaurant, Amigos, around seven-thirty. We were finished by around ten and we walked back to the hotel together."

Of course, as she started talking the evening flashed by in pictures and she was able to report, reasonably accurately, how she'd spent her time tonight. "Nicole Freedman, another National Sales Director, and her group ate at a pizza and pasta place across the street."

Luke's brows rose in silent question. Henderson's gaze remained steady on her face. "The main lobby, by the marble horse, is the usual meeting place for groups. I saw Nicole there. We left the hotel around the same time and walked to dinner, so I saw where her group ended up."

She went through the evening as well as she could remember, right up to the time she'd found Nicole.

She stopped and swallowed. It felt like she'd been talking a long time, hearing no other voice but her own. "And then I called 9-1-1."

"Can you remember everyone Nicole Freedman ate dinner with?"

"Of course. It was her team." Her head jerked up. "None of them would do...that."

"We only want to talk to them," he said soothingly.

"Did you know her well?" Henderson asked, speaking for the first time.

"We've both been with Lady Bianca for around fifteen years. I would call her a business acquaintance."

"Did she have any enemies?"

She heard again the echo of raised voices this afternoon. Her own and Nicole's.

Toni sighed. "As far as I know, only me."

CHAPTER 16

We understood Her by her sight; her pure and eloquent blood Spoke in her cheeks, and so distinctly wrought That one might almost say her body thought.

–John Donne

"You probably want to be careful saying things like that to a cop," Luke said.

She shook her head in a manic fashion so her loose curls slapped her cheeks. "I'm not being cute. Believe me. You'll find out soon enough. Ask about her enemies and you'll hear about the big fight Nicole and I had earlier today."

"What kind of fight?"

"Well, not a fistfight, obviously. It was more of an old fashioned shouting match. I said some things I shouldn't have."

"Like what?"

"I didn't threaten to kill her or anything. I didn't like the woman but I would never..."

"What was this fight about?"

She blew out a breath with enough force she could have extinguished a centenarian's birthday cake. "It all seems foolish now. Nicole is—was—in direct competition with me for a prestigious sales-volume based award. I didn't like her methods. I thought she was pressuring her associates to buy more stock than they needed or could afford. She thought I was trying to sabotage her." She thought back to the awful scene earlier that day. "We both said some things we shouldn't have. It wasn't one of my prouder moments."

She felt her brows squeeze together in a frown, thought screw Botox, and let herself wrinkle. "There's one more thing. She accused me of sending her threatening notes."

"What kind of notes?"

"I don't know. I didn't send them. At the time I thought she made them up, but now..."

"Email? Handwritten?"

"Email. She told Orin Shellenbach about them, too. He might know more."

Detective Henderson nodded. Frank. She hadn't known his name was Frank. "The 9-1-1 call came in just before midnight. What were you doing between ten and midnight?"

She noticed she was picking at her nail polish. It was a disgusting habit, one she'd willed herself out of when she began selling Lady Bianca and really taking care of her appearance. But now she couldn't seem to stop herself. A flake of pink polish and a lone diamond sparkle flicked from her nail and landed on her lemon-colored skirt.

"I came back to the hotel after dinner and Orin Shellenbach was waiting for me. He's the VP of—"

"We know who he is."

They must have talked to him after the first woman was murdered. She gulped. "He took me across the street to Starbucks for a meeting."

"Kind of late to have a business meeting."

"He'd heard about the fight. He wasn't exactly thrilled. He gave me a lecture." She had almost all the polish off her index fingernail. By scraping hard with her thumbnail, she lifted a ribbon of polish from her middle finger. "Some other women came in while we were talking so I got up. I really didn't want an audience and besides, we were done."

"So you left the coffee shop alone?"

"Yes. Then I went for a walk. I needed to cool down."

"Did anyone see you on this walk?"

Henderson was speaking and his voice gave nothing away. She knew his face wouldn't either but she wasn't looking up anytime soon. She had eight more nails to denude. "I don't think so. I was preoccupied, though, so I wasn't paying much attention. I got back around eleven forty-five, I guess—maybe closer to midnight—and I'd drunk all this iced tea. I wasn't going to make it to my room so I detoured into the washroom."

She swallowed. "And she was dead."

She felt panic bouncing around in her chest like a manic pinball. "She wasn't stiff like you read about. Rigor mortis."

"How do you know?"

"I told you already. I felt for a pulse in her neck." She mimed taking her own and felt her carotid artery smack her fingers so hard and fast she could have tap-danced to the beat. "Her skin was cool, but not cold."

She gulped. "Also, I did a really stupid thing."

"What?" he asked, sounding anything but astonished by the notion of her doing a stupid thing.

"I wasn't thinking straight. I thought about how she took such pride in her appearance and that she would never sit sprawled like that." Toni glanced up to find she had their full attention, and looked back down again. Another chunk of polish went flying. "I straightened her skirt and kind of pushed her knees and ankles together."

"You're right," Luke said conversationally. "You did do a really stupid thing."

"Sorry."

"Did you touch anything else?" Same conversational tone.

"No."

"The knife in her chest?"

Her head jerked up and she returned his gaze. "God, no. I can't believe someone killed her." Unaccountably, her voice started to wobble. It was one thing not to like a person, quite another to find them murdered.

Especially when a cop was looking at you as though his next words might be: "You have the right to remain silent."

The two detectives glanced at each other and did some kind of silent cop-speak, then Luke said, "Okay, Toni. That's enough for now. We may want to interview you again later."

She nodded.

He glanced again at his watch. "It's 2:03 a.m. The interview concludes."

They all walked out of the tiny interview room together. "Come on," Luke said. "I'll drive you home."

"You sure?" Henderson asked.

"Yeah. Get some sleep, Frank. I'll see you in the morning."

THEY GOT into the Taurus again; this time she was in the passenger seat. As they drove away from City Hall, she said, "Are you able to turn it off after you see death?"

He glanced at her then back to the road ahead. "No. You never get used to it. Some guys take a drink or two or pop a sleeping pill. Me, I restore old trucks. Sometimes I'm out in the garage all night." He made a wry face.

When they arrived back at the hotel, there were still a

number of police vehicles hanging around, but thankfully no media that she could spot.

The coroner's van was parked nearby so she knew Nicole was still up there in the bathroom. She shivered.

"Do you want me to walk you to your door?"

She nodded gratefully.

"Come on."

They walked into the hotel and straight for the elevators and he pushed the button. The door opened immediately and they stepped inside.

He punched the number and the doors closed. As the elevator rose, she said, "Will you go back down there? To the washroom?"

He nodded. "Try to think about something else," he suggested.

"I can't. Do you think the two deaths are connected?" she asked.

"It's the same MO, same location, similar murder weapon. That would be some series of coincidences, and I don't believe much in coincidence."

"But what links these two women?"

He looked as frustrated as she sounded. "Hell if I know."

Her stomach clenched. "Amy Neuman had nothing to do with Lady Bianca and Nicole Freedman didn't read mysteries. They lived miles apart. How could they be related?"

He made a sound that under other circumstances could have been termed a laugh. "Two murders within days of each other in the same location? Both female stabbing victims? There has to be a connection."

She was genuinely puzzled. "But what is it?"

"Nicole did Amy Neuman's makeover. We start there."

"Actually, Stacy Krump did her makeover—under Nicole's supervision."

"Was Stacy in the room the entire time?"

"I don't know. Probably she would have slipped into the washroom a few times to rinse brushes and get water for certain parts of the makeover."

"Leaving Nicole Freedman and Amy Neuman alone."

"But so what?"

He slumped against the wall of the elevator, right hand slipping inside his pants pockets. She waited and sure enough the tumbling of coins began. "We'll check into whether they knew each other before."

She nodded. It was the only thing that made sense. "But then who killed them?"

He looked at her levelly. "The only link between them is Stacy." He looked at her keenly. "What?"

"Nothing."

"You thought of something. I saw it on your face."

The elevator stopped, and the doors opened. "Stacy's the person Nicole and I had the fight about. That's all."

"She's the one Nicole forced into debt?"

They stepped out into the hallway.

"Come on, Luke. It was five grand. Not enough to break a person's knee caps over. Certainly not enough to kill for. Besides, all Stacy had to do was cancel the charge."

He nodded. "People do crazy things when they lose perspective. You'd be surprised. Or, maybe those women were randomly selected. Wrong place, wrong time. One sold Lady Bianca, the other had a Lady Bianca makeover. Could be some crazy who hates Lady Bianca. Maybe a former employee. If customers and sales reps start dying, it's going to hurt the reputation of the company."

"Well, if you go with the random selection theory, then maybe it's not Lady Bianca being targeted. But the hotel. The manager looked ill when I saw him earlier. What do you think this is going to do to the Weymouth's business?"

He stuck his hand back in his pocket and jingled the change he seemed to keep there for no other purpose. "We'll see an exodus of guests and a lot of cancelled bookings once word gets out. Could be an ex-employee of the hotel looking for revenge. We'll be checking into all employees and former employees, especially any who've been fired recently."

She swallowed. It felt like a marshmallow had lodged in her throat. "Or maybe there's a serial killer staying in the hotel." It was that thought that had made her too scared to go to her room alone.

"Random serial killers are much rarer than you'd think. You'll lock up behind me. You'll be okay."

"Do you think there will be more murders?"

He looked at her, his eyes dark and intense, and she realized he was angry. Probably at himself for not having caught the murderer yet. "I hope not."

They were almost at her door. "Like I said, try not to think about it if you can."

"What kind of trucks?"

"Hmm?"

"The trucks you work on when you can't sleep. What kind are they?"

His face softened, like he was talking about a favorite child. "Right now I'm working on a 1949 Chevy 6400, 2-ton. I've rebuilt the engine, now I'm working on the chassis."

"What color is it?"

His grin lit up his face. He didn't smile enough, she decided. He looked younger and definitely sexy. Even when the humor was at her expense. "That is such a girl question."

"In case you hadn't noticed, I am a girl."

In the dim lighting in the corridor his eyes were darker than sin. "Oh, I noticed." For a moment they stood there staring at each other.

Her heart hammered, but in a good way this time.

Then he pulled in a breath. “It’s red. G’night.”

“Good night.” She opened her door and entered her room, knowing he was watching to make sure she got inside all right.

And maybe for other reasons.

CHAPTER 17

Beauty to me is about being comfortable in your own skin. That or a kick-ass red lipstick.

–Gwyneth Paltrow

THE GLOWING NUMBERS on the clock taunted Toni until, in frustration, she stuck a pillow over the thing. Not that it was the light from the clock keeping her awake. There was plenty of light in her room since she was too scared to sleep in the dark. Every time she turned off all the lights she replayed the scene in the bathroom.

The horror of her discovery was still fresh but underneath the horror was a burning anger. Who killed Nicole? And why?

She hadn't liked the woman, but she understood the fierce urge to succeed in Nicole because she was honest enough to recognize that same quality in herself. Nicole had cut a lot of corners and hadn't always played fair, but she'd often been the person who spurred Toni on, a fact she was sure her rival didn't know.

When Toni felt too tired to send out a motivational email to her reps, when the thought of booking one extra party that month seemed like the last straw, she'd see Nicole's face in front of her and that would push her on.

She hadn't admired Nicole's principles or tactics, but she respected her work ethic. And the spur of competition that kept her sharp.

Who would kill her?

Usually she loved having her own room at the conference, but tonight a roommate would have been welcome. Somebody who could keep her company and maybe take her mind off her grisly discovery.

She flipped onto her back, then her side, then, with a huff, onto her front, but it was impossible. She got up and brewed a pot of the in-room coffee.

While it was gurgling and sputtering, she got out her lavender day planner. Flipped open to the notes section. Took out the diamond-encrusted pen her mom had given her for her last birthday and clicked the top.

She spent some time tapping the pen against the paper and got nothing for her trouble but a freckle-field of blue dots on the page. The only thing connecting the first murder and the second was that makeover. Stacy had given Amy Neuman her makeover. And Stacy had been very upset when Toni had seen her after lunch yesterday. But she sure didn't seem like the murdering type. And if there was a reasonable motive for her to kill Nicole, what possible reason could she have for killing Amy Neuman?

Because the woman gave a false name? Even if Stacy had been literary enough to figure out she'd been given a fake name by Amy, that happened to all of them from time to time. You shrugged and went on. You didn't kill.

However, for the moment, Stacy was the only still-living link between Nicole and Amy.

Reluctantly, she wrote Stacy's name on the top of her page. She couldn't imagine Stacy as a cold-blooded killer, but then people always said that about cold-blooded killers, that they'd never seemed the type.

Toni disfigured her page with a few more dots. Underlined Stacy's name.

Then she turned the page. Detective Marciano might not believe in coincidences. That was his business. And if he wanted to treat the two murders as related crimes, that was his business also. Toni was sorry for the first young woman, but her involvement began with Nicole's murder. She was under no obligation to consider the two deaths inseparably linked. She was an amateur detective. She could think whatever she wanted to.

She wrote Nicole's name at the top of the clean page. Underlined the name neatly.

Then she listed all of Nicole's reps that she'd seen at the conference so far. She was certain Melody could furnish her with all the names. Maybe they could help her figure out who hated Nicole enough to want her dead.

At last, she simply sat in front of the window watching the freeway get busier as morning crept up on Corvallis. She wondered which direction Luke lived and if he was even home yet. And if so, was he out in his garage tinkering with his red 1949 Chevy truck?

At five-thirty, she flipped on the TV news. And groaned. The second murder was the top story.

What a great birthday present for Lady Bianca. One of her top saleswomen was murdered and the media were knocking themselves out creating headlines that cleverly combined the words *killer* and *cosmetics*.

She was particularly grateful for her cosmetics training as

she stippled extra eye cream and then took a narrow, tapered brush and carefully trailed her thickest cream concealer over the circles under her eyes, careful to cover only the blue shadows. Concealer slapped all over the place tended to get cakey, and only drew attention to the circles.

It was more than simple vanity causing her to take extra care to camouflage the signs of a nearly sleepless night. Pride had her spine stiffening and her eyes snapping. She'd had a night to shiver and whine, she told her reflection firmly. Today she was going on the offensive.

She'd spent a lot of time while staring out the window wondering about those emails Nicole claimed she had received.

The police would have their own methods of detection, of course, highly sophisticated ones. They also had experience and training in policing. But they didn't know Lady Bianca the way she did. And she was going to use that inside knowledge to figure out what on earth was going on.

Once she'd made up her mind about something, Toni wasn't one to dawdle.

She dressed in a red suit, went a little more dramatic than usual on her makeup and swiped on her most confident red lipstick.

A woman who was going to war needed full war paint.

And coffee. A lot of coffee.

She headed downstairs on a caffeine-seeking missile.

"Toni!"

All Toni wanted was a cup of coffee. Just one inside her before she heard her name called in that desperate tone. She'd drunk the complimentary pot of coffee that came with the room between four and five a.m. That seemed like a long time ago now.

She'd hoped that by sneaking down here at six-thirty, the minute the coffee shop opened, she could refuel in relative peace.

But she knew that voice. She turned and put on her best guess at a delighted expression. "Morning, Melody."

"I'm so glad you're up early. I need someone to talk to."

"I didn't sleep too well last night. I need coffee."

"I can imagine. I'm sick about it. Just sick. How could anyone do that to poor Nicole?"

Icy claws pricked at Toni's skin. "How did you know about Nicole?"

Of course, that explained the outfit Melody was wearing. Where Toni had chosen defiant, *no murderer is getting me down*, red, Melody had gone with funereal black. The cheap fabric was pulling a little at the seams and emphasized Melody's pallor.

"It was on the news. I'm always up early. It's the dairy farmer's genes in me, I guess. My daddy always used to say, we could sleep in when the cows started sleeping in. Anyhow, I like to plan my day, visualize my goals and review my to-do list first thing. Then I get my hair done and my face on. I put the TV on while I was getting ready and I heard there'd been another murder here at the hotel."

"Killer Cosmetics Convention. I know. I can't believe how fast the media gets hold of stories."

"They all have scanners and things. They eavesdrop on the police channel."

"But they didn't give out her name."

"No. They didn't say who was killed, only that the second suspicious death in a week had occurred right here at the hotel, during the Lady Bianca conference. So I ran down to Nicole's room. I thought she'd want to know right away. I knocked on the door, and a police officer opened it." Her voice wobbled, and she bit her lip. "And that's how I found out it was her."

Since it was obvious the woman was going to keep talking, Toni resumed walking toward the coffee shop and Melody stayed right with her.

"I didn't know what to do. I couldn't stay in my room or I'd have gone crazy. So I came down here, and now I know that I was led here."

"Where's your husband?"

"He's upstairs." Her pretty face creased. "He's upset. He wants us to pack up and go home." She took an actual linen handkerchief from her bag and dabbed at her eyes. "We never fight, but we had words. He's worried for my safety, I know that. But Nicole would have wanted me to go on."

They'd reached the coffee shop, thank goodness. And, as Toni had guessed, they were the first customers.

"Morning, ladies," said a far too cheery server. "Sit anywhere and I'll be right with you."

"Bring coffee. A whole pot."

"Coming right up."

"What am I going to do without her?" Melody wailed. "She's been my mentor and my best friend. I—"

"Thank you," Toni said with real gratitude when their server arrived with a silver carafe of coffee. She poured the beautiful, black stream of *Awake* into the thick china cup in front of Toni. Then she filled Melody's cup before placing the pot in the middle of the table and taking two menus from under her arm and planting them in front of the two women.

Toni took a tongue-scalding sip of coffee before answering the woman across from her. "You were Nicole's second-in-command, I know it's going to be hard for you, but you've got to stay strong for the rest of the team. It's what Nicole would want."

"I'm a wreck about Nicole and I'm so nervous around the police. They're going to interview me, aren't they?" She took a sip of coffee and then put the cup down with a clack. "I must be in shock. I don't even drink coffee."

"It's okay. Maybe you can even help the police solve her murder. You knew her better than anyone."

Melody picked up the menu and opened it. "I should get some tea. Some kind of herbal tea to calm the nerves." Then she put the menu down again. Toni had never seen her so agitated.

"And, of course, you were with Nicole last night." She remembered seeing them at the crowded meeting area in the lobby.

"That's right. We went for dinner with the rest of our team last night. We got back around ten, I guess. I went straight up to my room." She got the words out fast, almost as though waving an alibi in front of Toni.

"Did Nicole go up with you?"

"No. She said she had an errand to take care of."

Gooseflesh was breaking out all over Toni's skin, she could feel it prickling like a mounting fever. Had her timing been only slightly off, she could have walked in on the murder in progress, and everybody knew what happened to the accidental witness. She shivered and drank more coffee. If only her brain wasn't so fogged from shock and lack of sleep, maybe she could think more clearly.

"Any idea what the errand was?"

Melody caught the waitress's attention and asked for cranberry tea with a slice of fresh lemon.

"No. She didn't say."

"Did you see where she went?"

"No." Melody polished the three pieces of silverware at her place with her napkin and replaced them carefully. "I saw her pull her cell phone out, though."

"Did she make a call or receive one?"

Melody shook her head. "I turned my head to call out something to her but she was kind of far away. I just remember that she had her cell phone in her hand. Looked like she was getting ready to start talking on it."

"Hopefully the police can pull the records and find out who she called. And who called her."

Melody's menu lost her attention suddenly. "Are you saying the police can know about all her calls?"

"I think so."

Melody went so pale all of a sudden that her blush stood out in two perfectly symmetrical apples on her cheekbones. "Can they hear what we said? You know, like they say every email you ever send is out there somewhere. Is it the same with cell phone calls?"

"I don't think so. Why?"

"Well, I don't want to speak ill of the dead, but Nicole wasn't exactly shy about giving her opinion. When we talked on the phone, sometimes she would say things about people—and I'd really be happy if no one ever had to hear those conversations. I mean, it's not like I was bad-mouthing anyone, but you know how it is. It could sound like I was agreeing with her."

"I'm guessing I was one of the people she bad-mouthed?"

Melody looked around. "Where is that waitress with my tea?"

She doubted very much that the police could obtain transcripts of Nicole's cell phone calls but she wasn't in a hurry to reassure Melody of that fact. "Who else did she trash talk, Melody?"

"I don't want to tell tales out of school. The woman's dead. I shouldn't have even said anything. I'm all messed up, right now, is all."

"The police are going to want a list of any enemies Nicole might have had."

The black curls bounced as Melody shook her head—a pudgy Snow White trying to refuse the apple. "She didn't have any enemies. She was assertive and she didn't let anything stand in her way so sometimes people didn't understand her, but she had a really good heart."

Fortunately, the waitress arrived at that moment with the tea and both women took a moment. Melody to squeeze lemon and a hint of honey into her cup and Toni to consider what to say next.

Finally, Melody said, "I want to ask you something."

"Sure. Anything."

"Would you sit with me when the police interview me?"

"Me? But—"

"I'd ask Nicole, but—"

"Right."

"I know it's silly, but I'm scared to talk to them by myself and you won't let them bully me. You can be like my lawyer."

"I'm not legally trained, Mel. Do you think you need a lawyer?"

"What? Oh, Lord, no. I only meant I want someone who's there to hold my hand." She bit her lip. "I mentioned it to Thomas, but he's so upset, I doubt he'll come."

"Of course, I'll be there for you." She wasn't sure the detectives on the case would be thrilled to have her present, but she figured that wasn't her problem.

And she was so deeply involved now that it felt only right she should be part of the investigation.

CHAPTER 18

It is better to be beautiful than to be good, but it is better to be good than to be ugly.–Oscar Wilde

Detective Marciano seemed less than delighted when Toni walked into Longhorn B at ten o'clock that morning with a nervous Melody beside her.

"Ms. Diamond," he said. "What a surprise."

"Melody asked me to sit in. Is it okay?"

He glanced at Henderson and something in that impassive countenance must have been visible to him that wasn't to her. "Sure."

They'd barely settled to the task when Thomas Feckler walked into the room. "Sorry, I'm late, honey."

Melody stretched out a hand to him and beamed. "That's okay. I'm just glad you're here. Detectives, this is my husband, Thomas."

"Are we waiting for anyone else or can we get started?" Marciano asked.

Thomas Feckler settled beside his wife and then noticed Toni sitting to the side. "Toni," he said in a polite version of a "What the hell are you doing here?" tone.

Melody said, "I wasn't sure you could make it, so I asked Toni to come with me." She giggled and looked toward the two cops. "I'm a little nervous."

Thomas Feckler's expression cleared. "How nice of you to come and support Melody."

Having done her best to interview Melody over breakfast, she had to admire the way Marciano got so much more information out of the woman.

When he asked, "Tell me about Nicole." Melody took out her linen handkerchief, looked at it and put it back into her bag. "Nicole was great. But she could be pretty hard on people."

"Go on."

"She really expected the best from all of us and if we didn't reach our goals she took it kind of personal." She swallowed. Touched her throat. "Is it okay if I have a glass of water?"

"Of course." Marciano started to rise but her husband was already out of his seat and headed for the jug of ice water and the glasses the hotel had set out. The room was silent but for the glugging of water and clattering of ice into the glass. He put the water in front of his wife. All his movements were quick and efficient, yet unobtrusive. He was the perfect type to be in the hospitality business, Toni thought, shaking her head when he silently offered her a glass of water before taking his seat once more.

Melody sipped her water. Ice tinkled against the glass. Everybody waited.

Luke spoke. "You said that if you didn't reach your goals, Ms. Freedman took that personally. What did you mean by that?"

"She'd get mad at us. Make us feel like we were personally letting her down.

"Sometimes she could say some harsh things, but I know it was because she wanted so much for all of us."

Toni kept her snort contained, but it wasn't easy. Nicole wasn't one of those people who achieved sainthood the second they shuffled off this mortal coil. Toni didn't wish her dead, but that woman had been nasty.

"Some of the girls couldn't handle it and they left."

"Would you be able to give us the names of the women who quit in the last year?"

"Oh, but none of them would—I mean—sure. I'm sure I can find all the names and addresses. There aren't that many."

The door to Longhorn B was closed, but Toni could still hear activity outside. She realized it was the changeover time between conference sessions. No doubt the gossip mill was churning full force with the shocking news about Nicole. No doubt her name was being mentioned pretty frequently too. She wondered if the top brass in the company were considering canceling the remainder of the conference and hoped fiercely that they wouldn't do that. It seemed important somehow for Nicole, and everything she had stood for, to continue.

"Is there anything at all that might help us in our search for Nicole's killer?"

"Nicole's killer. I can't stand hearing those words. I keep wondering if there's a serial killer in the hotel. What if I'm next? I was the only person who saw those threatening emails."

Toni glanced at Luke and their gazes connected. So the notes weren't invented by Nicole.

Melody's voice was rising and starting to wobble. She drank water and Toni could see her hands shaking. She held one out and her husband clasped it in his.

"I made Thomas stay on with me. He was supposed to go home this morning, but I made him promise he'll stay with me until the end of the convention. He thinks I should go home. But I have to stay. Nicole—"

"You said she showed you some emails?"

"We all have our own email addresses and websites at Lady Bianca. These messages seemed to be coming from the head office. But they weren't."

"What did the messages say?" Henderson asked in his quiet, calm way. Toni was so worked up by the news she could feel herself leaning forward in her chair wanting to shriek at Melody to hurry up and spill everything, but Henderson sounded exactly the same when asking about threatening notes as he had when he'd asked Melody to confirm her home address and contact numbers.

"They said to stop stealing the lives and money of her consultants or she'd be sorry."

"What do you think the notes referred to?"

"Well, it's the same as what she and Toni were fighting about yesterday—" She gulped and turned a panicked face to Toni. "Sorry, Toni."

"It's okay." And she'd have to live with that for the rest of her life. The last words she'd ever spoken to the soon-to-be-dead woman had been hurled in the heat of fury.

"I think someone was really jealous of our success." Her eyes glowed when she talked about Nicole and the team. "We were poised for such amazing success. I'm so grateful to Nicole for all she did for me."

"Any idea who was sending the notes?"

"No. She got a techie friend of hers to trace them, but it was hopeless. He said the hacker knew what he was doing."

"Maybe the police would have had better luck," Luke said. "Did she save the messages?"

"I'm not sure. I doubt it. She was big on positive thinking and removing anything negative from her life. She probably got rid of them. But you could check her computer."

"She didn't print them out and keep a copy?"

"I don't know. She might have."

Toni opened her mouth and shut it again. She was dying to know why Nicole showed her the notes.

"Why did Nicole show you the notes?" Luke asked and Toni felt like kissing him.

"She wanted to know if I'd received any. And also to brainstorm on who might be sending them." She took another sip of water. "I think she kind of wanted to share them, too, you know? They were kind of freaky."

"Freaky how?"

"Sort of polite, but scary."

"And did anyone else get them to your knowledge?"

She shook her head. "No."

"When were they sent? And how many were there?"

"She didn't tell me about them until a couple of months ago. She said she'd been getting these strange messages but she didn't say how many. I know she's had two or three more since then."

"When was the last one?"

"A week ago. Right before we left for this convention.

"Was this message the same as the rest?"

She shook her head. Picked up her now almost empty water glass. Put it down and shoved her hands over her eyes. "I should have made her go to the cops. I know I should have. The last note said, 'A person like you doesn't deserve to live.'"

CHAPTER 19

Beauty is the bait, which, with delight, allures man to enlarge his kind.

–Socrates

THAT NIGHT, Toni did something she almost never did.

She walked into a bar alone. She'd had a lousy day. Not even the lunch celebrating Lady Bianca's birthday, complete with a video message from Lady B. herself had been enough to lift her spirits. There were too many empty spots at the lunch tables, too many reps abandoning the conference and those who stayed weren't exactly on top form.

Toni walked into the dimly-lit lobby lounge and headed straight for the dark gleaming wood of the bar itself with its neatly spaced line up of upholstered stools. She sat on the middle one and ordered a glass of white wine.

She'd barely tasted her drink when a man took the stool beside her.

She ignored him, until he called to the bartender. "Excuse me," he said. "What would a recently-accused murder suspect order to drink?"

She turned to him. His face was sensitive and intelligent, his hair a mop of black curls that looked somehow Irish and poetic. He wore a brown corduroy jacket and a shirt that was open at the neck revealing dark chest hair. "Are you joking?"

"No. I am a murder suspect. If you want me to move away, of course I'll understand. I could sit in that dark corner over there." He gestured to the farthest recesses.

The bartender wasn't interested in guessing what he should drink so he sighed and said, "Cognac."

"So, did you?" she asked. "Kill her?"

"Kill Amy Neuman?" He shook his head and stared down at the dark wood. "No. She was a dear friend. I hurt her emotionally, but I'd never harm her. She loved me, you see."

Bad luck for Amy. This guy was exactly the sort of man who'd tell a woman in a bar about his conquests. What a jackass.

"I'm Joseph Mandeville," he said. "My friends call me Joe."

"Right. The guy who wrote a book about committing the perfect murder."

He looked absurdly pleased that she knew who he was. "And then gets involved in one."

"I'm Toni Diamond. I'm an independent..." She was too tired for her usual spiel. "I sell makeup."

He frowned into his glass. "I hurt her— And now she's gone. I will always regret that she left this world harboring ill feelings toward me."

Oh, boy. Hardly an egotist at all. The poor woman was horribly murdered, and he was worrying about whether he'd be kept awake at night because of his less than gallant behavior.

"Well, you write about murder, maybe you can also help solve them. An English teacher who reads mysteries and a woman who sells makeup both die. The only connection is that the first victim had a makeover in the second victim's room."

Joseph Mandeville shook his head at her in a chiding way. "You've jumped to conclusions, Toni. Remember, 'When the probable has been excluded, the improbable remains.'"

"Is that a quote?"

"Yes. Sherlock Holmes."

She shook her head. "What is it with you people and Holmes?" She sipped her drink. "Probable, improbable. Everything's starting to seem improbable. If not impossible. If it weren't for the actual corpses, I wouldn't believe there'd been two murders myself."

"Maybe there is no connection."

"You think the two murders could be a coincidence? That's what I thought, but the police are convinced they're linked."

"Coincidences do happen. In spite of the old wives' tale to the contrary, lightning does strike the same spot twice. It's unusual, but statistically possible. Lightning has no memory of where it struck." He paused to take another healthy sip of his drink. "The number of real-life murders I have studied have led me to believe that anything can and does happen. It's possible there is no connection."

"So, you didn't know Nicole Freedman." She paused, glancing sideways at him. "Did you?"

"Lord, no." He shuddered. "Those makeup women terrify me." Then, realizing to whom he was speaking, he added, "Present company excepted, of course."

She smiled, feeling unaccountably better now she had someone to talk to who really understood what she was going through. "We're not so bad once you get to know us."

"Especially one on one." He turned his head just so and a lock of poetically Irish hair fell artistically across his brow. If her mom could see him coming on to Toni she'd say, "Well, ain't he just the tom-cat's kitten?"

Even if she'd had any interest in this guy, all she had to do was remember what happened to the last woman he was intimate with and her interest was squashed.

"They searched my room, you know. Went through my things."

She imagined unknown cops pawing through her stuff and was horrified. "How awful." Then, because she always spoke when she should shut up, she asked, "Did they find anything?"

"No. But I've agreed to hand over some correspondence. It's obvious her husband killed her, and her love for me is the motive, so the letters are evidence. Amy had a lovely way with words. She wrote some passionate letters and cards as well as emails. I couldn't bear to destroy them. Horrible to think of strangers reading them out of context." He stared into his drink. Brooding. "I had led the police to believe we'd only just met here. Trying to be a gentleman in my own hopeless way." Or protect himself from suspicion?

"So you didn't just meet?"

"No. We had, in fact, enjoyed a passionate, physical relationship. I believe she misunderstood my intentions. I'm a man of the world. I travel a great deal and meet a number of interesting women." He glanced up, let his gaze travel lower than her face. "Such as yourself. But it's not in my nature to settle or to tie myself to one woman. She misunderstood. Had already started divorce proceedings."

"She left her husband for you?" Poor, poor Amy.

"No. She left her husband because the marriage was over. I was a convenient excuse and I like to think I helped her get over the rough emotional ground."

"I'm guessing she didn't see it that way?"

"You'd make a good detective, Toni," he said with a slight smile. "No, she did not. She was angry and upset and the nights we'd planned together here never happened." He shook his head. "She was never in my room, which was at least helpful in keeping me from being arrested for her murder."

"Are the police making you stay in the area?"

"No. After the mystery readers conference ends tomorrow, I'm free to leave." He took another sip of his drink. "I intend to stay, however. It's not every day that a true crime writer is on the scene for a double murder. And implicated in one of them."

"Sounds like you've got your next book." And she had a feeling more strangers would end up reading poor Amy's impassioned letters.

He shrugged. "I didn't ask for this to happen, but I'd be a fool not to take advantage."

"But what about Amy's—"

"Oh, no. My least favorite cop just walked in." He drained the drink. He rose, gave her a practiced come to bed look. "I have a copy of my book upstairs if you'd like to see what I mean about coincidence?"

Smooth as a greased pig. "Thanks. But I've had all the excitement I can stand for one day."

He took the brush off in good humor. "Well, it was a pleasure to meet you, Toni. I'm in Room 1213 if you change your mind." He held out his hand and she shook it.

From the other direction, Luke was approaching. He gave Joseph the barest hint of a curt nod before taking the seat on the other side of Toni.

He didn't waste time on greetings. "How do you know Mandeville?"

"I don't. He was hitting on me."

"Huh."

"I see the hand cream's working for you."

He shook his head at her. "Why would you think that?"

"Because your hands don't have dirt under the nails. And the skin's smoother."

"Maybe I didn't work on my truck last night."

And maybe she'd had a full night's sleep. "Why can't you just admit that our products are great?"

"Because I know you. You'll sell me a pedicure set for men."

He looked as tired as she felt. "We don't sell pedicure sets for men, silly." She glanced at him from under her lashes. "But there's a *Moisturizer for Him* that would—"

"No!"

She shrugged. One day he'd learn to love his skin. Maybe not today, but one day. "Joseph Mandeville said something interesting just now."

"I doubt it."

She ignored the sarcasm. "He quoted Holmes, saying that 'When the probable has been excluded, the improbable remains.'"

"Yeah? I got a quote for you. 'Everybody lies.' Especially Mandeville."

She felt as though she'd been smacked. It was at that moment that she began to see a glimmer of possibility in the darkness of puzzlement.

"Everybody lies." She leaned forward toward Luke. "If we stop believing everything that can't be proven, then it all looks different, doesn't it?"

He looked at her as though she hadn't been getting enough sleep lately, which was true. "What exactly are you talking about?"

"I'm talking about things we've been assuming that could be completely the opposite."

He scooped peanuts out of the communal bowl on the counter in front of him and popped one in his mouth. "You got something you want to share with the rest of the class? We can use all the fresh ideas you've got."

"Hmm? Oh, no. I was thinking about business. My business, I mean, not yours. Sorry."

The bartender came by. "What can I get you?"

He ordered a beer, motioned to her drink with his brows raised but she shook her head. His badge gleamed on his belt as he turned.

He acknowledged the beer with nod, took a drink, all the while keeping his gaze on her. "I can see the gears turning."

"If you stop believing everything that can't be proven, things can start to look different."

"You got any specific things in mind?"

"You can't prove there's a connection between Amy Neuman and Nicole Freedman. It's improbable that the murders have nothing to do with each other, but not impossible. And there are some things I'm going to check on. Lady Bianca stuff."

He didn't look entirely convinced but neither did he look as though he were going to push her, which was just as well. The notion that had smacked her was still vague and she wasn't anywhere near sure that she was right.

"Any luck finding those threatening emails?"

He rubbed a hand over his face. He was as tired as she was, she thought. "Nothing on her laptop here. Henderson's driven to her home to see if there's anything there."

"Henderson drove all that way?"

"He's meeting some tech guys there, but we wanted someone from our department on scene to check out Nicole's home."

"Isn't it awfully far?"

"About a four hour drive."

"Huh. I never knew Nicole and I lived so close together."

"All those tea parties you missed."

Since she couldn't possibly explain that she was going to miss Nicole in a strange way, she didn't bother answering.

"What did you think of the emails as Melody described them?"

"The word creepy springs to mind."

He shifted on his seat to get a better view of her face. "The wording."

"We're assuming Melody remembers that one email word for word?"

"Seemed like she was repeating something she'd memorized, yeah."

He sipped his beer and glanced over the room, as a reflex action she bet, who was here? Where might potential trouble start? She wondered if he ever truly relaxed.

He asked, "Did Nicole have a boyfriend?"

"You asked Melody that this morning. She said no."

"Now I'm asking you. You see things other people miss."

She was absurdly flattered by the compliment, which seemed more sincere because of the casual way he said it. Like he was merely relating a fact.

"I don't think so. She got divorced a few years back and as far as I know her heart belonged to Lady Bianca."

"What about her body?"

There was a silent ping in her mind as the obvious truth hit her. "She had sex the night she died, didn't she?"

"Why would you think that?" He watched her face.

Once more her mind flipped back to finding the woman dead. She replayed the scene. Again. "She wasn't wearing pantyhose. I noticed when I pushed her knees and ankles together." The sound of tinkling piano keys intruded. The nightly pianist was starting his first set off with *The Girl from Ipanema*. "And when I smoothed her skirt, I didn't feel a panty line." She gulped a little wine. "Do you think whoever she slept with killed her?"

He shifted in his seat. "I think you should be careful about spreading these opinions of yours."

"I wouldn't—"

"And of getting too friendly with Mandeville."

"Mandeville? But he—"

"How many men do you see around the hotel, Toni? It's a sea of estrogen."

"Okay, Mandeville was sleeping with Amy Neuman." At his look she rolled her eyes. "He told me. But he didn't even know Nicole."

Luke popped another peanut in his mouth, his eyes steady on hers. "We only have his word for that. He likes to pick up women in bars."

"I turned him down." And exactly why had she been so eager to tell him that?

He glanced around the bar again and his face relaxed into a grin. He nodded in recognition to an extremely colorful older woman sitting at one of the round tables for four with a much more conventional-looking senior. She raised her glass to him. Some amber-colored liquor. Scotch maybe.

She spoke to her friend and then motioned them over. Luke glanced at her. "Do you mind if we join them?"

Since when were she and Luke a *we*?

He introduced her to the colorful woman whose name was Miss Barnes, "Call me Helen," and her friend Betty Tait. The pair of them were with the mystery writers conference.

"Helen, you were an English teacher, I believe?"

She nodded. "For forty years. Everything from remedial composition to advanced English lit."

"I'm interested in what you think of this wording in an email, hypothetically, of course."

"Of course." She leaned forward. All three women did, in fact.

He quoted, "A person like you doesn't deserve to live."

Her brown eyes snapped to his and Toni immediately got that hot, sick feeling like she'd forgotten to do her homework and was about to be nailed. She even held a pencil in her hand and rolled it between her fingers as though getting ready to tear apart an essay. "That's it? No salutation? No closing?"

"That's it."

She blinked slowly, and the iridescent green shadow on her lids glinted like wrinkled opals. When she opened her eyes she said, "Interesting phrasing for a threat. Passive construction. Vague subject. Ends with an infinitive." She swirled her drink and then took a sip. They all waited. "In the days when I taught school, if a student had a problem with another child he might scrawl, 'You die' on his locker. 'I'll get you', and then refer to him by some vicious, socially demeaning epithet. You know the ones."

"I can guess."

Her jaw worked up and down. "Angry, visceral, blunt nouns, active verbs. This is almost at a distance. Polite, even. Certainly unusual. I'm no psychiatrist, though after forty years of teaching high school I feel like one. It could be this person's a foreigner so their English is learned from a textbook. Or they are very uncomfortable with their anger, so they try to distance themselves from it. Passive aggressive."

Luke nodded.

"I can't even tell if it's a male or a female. But when those types finally explode, they tend to make a mess."

"Yeah."

"Well, Detective, is that your strongest clue?" Helen sounded worried as well she might. Toni noticed she was wearing one of the *No, I don't want a Lady Bianca makeover* buttons on her forest green cardigan. Even so, Toni adored her on sight. She was like the funhouse mirror version of a sweet old lady. She smoked, based on the nicotine stains on her fingers and her teeth, she drank, she wore the most bizarre color palette of makeup Toni'd ever seen, and she'd stuck a black bow in her red wig. "You won't solve a murder with one email."

He smiled at the extraordinarily colorful woman. "Miss Barnes. What I need is some help from your fictional friends."

She chuckled, a deep-chested sound that veered away from a coughing fit at the last second. "Holmes, or Lord Peter Whimsey or Miss Marple would have the mystery wrapped up by now, the killer confessed and the tea on to boil. You're sadly behind schedule."

"But the author would obligingly leave a trail of clues for the plodding gumshoe to follow."

She shook her head and an aviary of bright birds hanging from her ears took flight. "Ah, don't forget the absence of clues, Detective."

He narrowed his eyes. "Silver Blaze?"

"Very good. The curious incident of the dog in the night-time." She nodded at him approvingly.

"I feel like a toad in a dryer trying to figure out what you two are talking about," Toni said, looking from one to the other.

"Sherlock Holmes." Helen Barnes explained in her English teacher way. Again with the Holmes. "One of his most famous cases. A vital clue was the dog that didn't bark when it should have."

The other three at the table all had that reminiscent look people get when they share a memory. Toni figured she just looked confused. "Why didn't it bark?"

"Because the dog knew the villain. So it had no reason to bark. A vital clue and a famous one because, of course, sometimes what's not present is as significant as what is."

"You mean, no clue can be a clue?"

"Exactly."

"Wow. It's kinda like one of my favorite sayings to my sales reps. 'A No isn't a No until the potential customer says that word. You'd be amazed at how rarely women say no. They'll give excuses like 'I'm too busy,' or 'I don't wear much make-up,' which are all great openers for a motivated salesperson to turn that excuse into a sale. Imagine using that same technique to solve a murder."

"I'm saying No," Helen said, pointing to the button on her sweater. But there was challenge in her tone.

And Toni loved a challenge. "You're not saying 'No,' Helen. You're wearing that button hoping to stop a sales rep from approaching you. That's not the same thing at all."

"All right then. Ask me if I want a makeover."

Toni sat back. It was so nice to be able to focus on something positive, like a sales challenge, than to obsess about death.

She smiled. "I'm not a fool, Helen. Besides, I love your style. I wouldn't change a thing." She turned to Helen's friend, Betty. "I love everything about your friend's style. It's unique to her. Of course, her skin is dry. And since she stopped smoking, it needs extra moisture. We have a wonderful lip liner that stops the lipstick from bleeding. But that's only going to improve what already works."

She pulled her chair back, "Well—"

"How do you know I just quit smoking?"

"You've got nicotine stains on your fingers but you don't smell of smoke. You're chewing gum and rolling that pencil where your cigarette used to be. My mama did the same thing when she quit. Only with an eyebrow pencil."

It wasn't what you heard that mattered. It was what you didn't hear. Her mind flashed back to Nicole and tried to veer away, wimp that she was. But Toni found if she concentrated on trying to figure out who had killed her rival, the horror of finding the woman's body moved to the back of her brain. She knew it was only in temporary storage, but right now she'd take any relief. All she knew was she had some thinking to do. So, she smiled at the eager mystery buffs and said, "You know, my brain feels thicker than candy floss right now. I didn't get much sleep last night. I think I'll go on up. Good night, ladies. Night, Luke."

"Night."

"Wait."

She turned back and Helen said, "This lip liner of yours, does it really work?"

"You won't believe the difference. The liner keeps the lipstick right where it belongs, on your lips."

"All right," the gravelly voice said. "You'd better give me your card." Then she looked fierce. "But I'm not having a makeover."

"I wouldn't dream of it." She took out her cards and handed one to each of the women. She didn't even let her triumphant grin out until she'd turned once more toward the lobby and had started walking away.

Helen Barnes was one of those old women who had no idea how far her voice carried. Or else she didn't care. As Toni walked away from the table she clearly heard her say, "Speaking of dogs that don't bark, Detective."

His reply was thankfully much softer but she thought he said, "Mind your own business, Helen."

CHAPTER 20

The inmate of a house in which a mysterious murder had occurred was rather an interesting object.

–Anna Katharine Green

As Toni approached the elevator hall where a small crowd of Lady Bianca women waited, the conversation suddenly snuffed. She supposed she couldn't blame them for gossiping about her and Nicole, and the gruesome death, but the heavy silence only added to the weight she already carried.

And good for them—these were the gals who had stayed. They were all back from socializing. The networking and sisterhood were an important part of the conference's success and, decent women that they were, they soon began chattering about different subjects than the one on everybody's mind.

Two women began chatting quietly about their kids' baseball teams, and another couple began sharing eBay success stories.

The elevator arrived and the doors opened. The group filed in and, as the doors were about to close, Luke Marciano jogged into the elevator.

He nodded politely to all of them. “Ladies.”

“Which floor would you like?” one of the eBay sellers asked him.

“It’s already lit up, thanks.”

He seemed to quell all conversation as effectively as she had, so Toni never found out whether, with two out and the bases loaded, the Dynamos beat the Tigers, or what happened in the final, frenzied minutes of bidding for the vintage costume jewelry that had belonged to the eBay woman’s aunt.

By the time the elevator reached her floor, there were only four of them left. Luke hadn’t said a word to her or even glanced her way. In fact, he’d spent the entire ride watching the floor indicator light up as they rose.

At the fourteenth floor, she stepped out. Surprise, surprise, he followed.

After the elevator doors closed, he joined her.

“You staying at the hotel?” she asked him.

“Seeing you safely to your room.”

For some reason, he didn’t make her feel entirely safe. Not that she felt unsafe, more unsettled, since she had no idea of his intentions or her own feelings on the matter.

They arrived at her room and he waited while she fished out her key. She glanced up at him, half amused and half irritated. “Are you going to come in and check under the bed?”

“Yes.”

She rolled her eyes. “Fine.”

She opened her hotel room door and they both entered. She flipped on a light and the door shut behind them with a whisper.

“Did you work on your 1949 truck last night?”

He made a face. “Yeah. What did you do?”

"Well, I didn't sleep like a baby. I got out a notebook and made a list of people Nicole works with and people she's ticked off. It's quite a long list."

"I wouldn't mind a copy."

"Sure. Any news on the knife that was..." She mimed a stabbing motion to her own chest. It was easier somehow than saying the words aloud. "Did she, um," Toni didn't even know how to phrase her question. "Was it quick? Her death?"

Those espresso-dark eyes didn't so much as flicker.

He nodded once. "Knife pierced the heart and sliced the aorta. She'd have been dead in minutes."

"Some of the girls think there's a serial killer."

"I know. Media are playing up the angle, too. Nicole Freedman wasn't killed by some random psycho. We're pretty sure her killer is still here. It is possible they'll kill again."

She shivered. As she was sure he'd meant her to.

"So you think it could be a woman?"

"Absolutely."

"Don't you have to be pretty strong to kill someone with a knife?"

"Both murder weapons came from the hotel kitchen," he said. "They were razor sharp and made for chopping big cuts of meat. A frail old lady probably couldn't manage the deed but a reasonably fit woman, sure."

"Oh, how awful. Were there any fingerprints or anything?"

He shook his head.

"But, the knife we found in the kitchen that day, when Lucy was having a fit, was the one used on Amy Neuman. The killer dumped it in the industrial dishwasher, presumably on his way out after killing her."

"He put the knife in the dishwasher, like he'd finished carving the Sunday roast?" Somehow that detail, and the casual attitude the killer showed to his victim, added a touch of evil to an already gruesome deed. "How do you know it was the murder weapon if it went through the dishwasher?"

He walked past the bed. "We won't know about DNA evidence until next week, but the hilt made a mark on Amy's body and the boning knife matches. Blade's the right width and there's a slice mark on one of the ribs that matches the blade. Bottom line, the Medical Examiner is ninety percent certain it's the murder weapon."

"And the knife that killed Nicole?"

"A carving knife that went missing some time after dinner last night."

He walked into the bathroom, flipped on the light and checked the room, even behind the shower curtain. His thorough search of her room was both reassuring and terrifying.

She tried to imagine walking into a hotel kitchen, taking a knife and stabbing someone with it. "The curious incident of the dog in the nighttime," she said.

His gaze settled on her face as he came out of the bathroom. "I thought you didn't read Sherlock Holmes."

"I was thinking about what your mystery reading lady friend said about the absence of clues. No dog barking. This is sort of the same, isn't it?" She set her conference bag down beside the desk.

"Not following."

"Well, any old person can't walk into a hotel kitchen and borrow a chef's knife, right? How come nobody noticed or said anything?"

The coins started jingling in his pocket, a clear sign he was thinking.

"In Silver Blaze the dog doesn't bark because he knows the villain."

"So, maybe your killer works in the kitchen or had a good reason to be in there. Like waiters, busboys, dishwashers. They must hire a ton of casual staff during the big conferences."

"Sure, but it's an easy area to get in and out of. And lots of conventions have food committees. I bumped into you there."

She nodded, reluctantly. "We hire a company to organize the convention for us, but there are always a few reps helping organize the food. I served on it once. You would not believe how many food allergies people have. Then there are the vegetarians, the vegans, the diabetics, the low salt diets. It's a nightmare. But it still seems strange to me that no one noticed someone walk in and take a knife. Particularly after the first murder."

"Sure. Could be a connection to the kitchen. Or maybe the killer waited until nobody was around. Lady Bianca's still the closest connection between the two victims."

She thought back to the first murder. "Pretty bold, walking into the kitchen with a bloody knife."

"This killer is definitely bold. Or desperate."

"But not hiding in my room."

His eyes crinkled in a half smile. "No. But you and Nicole had a lot in common. You don't go anywhere alone. Make sure you have your flunkies around, people you trust. And watch your back. I mean it." He walked to the door.

She followed.

"Do you always take such good care of your suspects?"

The smile still lurked deep in his eyes. He had great eyes—liquid, sexy dark chocolate. "You're not a suspect."

Then he pulled her to him and kissed her. Not long, or hard, or passionately, but soft and swift. A tease and a promise.

"Lock up behind me."

She was so stunned she could only nod.

CHAPTER 21

False coins have often lustre, though they want weight.

–Samuel Johnson

EVERYBODY LIES. Luke had thrown the statement out carelessly enough, but she felt as though he'd given her the key to the maze in which she found herself.

Well, if not a key, at least a hint as to which was the correct path.

She sat up in bed, gripping her knees, sleepless again. Of course people lied, they lied all the time. Not always with evil intent. People lied to protect themselves, someone else, the hearer's feelings. They lied to make themselves seem more successful, wealthier, more attractive. But whatever the motive, lies hid the truth.

Toni had no way of knowing who was lying about what or why, but if she believed only what was absolutely provable, then perhaps she might see through the fog of deception she felt all around her.

She, of all people, should have understood that from the beginning. Her profession depended upon covering the truth with illusion. Shaving years off a face with the right cream, hiding blemishes with concealer that mimicked perfect skin, lip liners and glosses that lied about the shape and plumpness of a mouth, why, with the right palette, she could change the appearance of a client's eye color.

She had to assume that she'd fallen for some pretty faces. Pretty lies dressed up. Now it was time to get out the makeup remover and scrub down to the naked truth.

She pulled out her notebook and went back to her list of every person she could think of who might have means, motive and opportunity to kill Nicole. Reluctantly, she added the name Joseph Mandeville. He could easily have met her in the hotel. Nicole wasn't married anymore, but Toni doubted very much she did completely without male companionship. Besides, she'd had sex the night she died. And how many men were even in the hotel with Lady Bianca taking up most of the rooms?

Unlike Luke and his crew, she didn't have to follow any rules but her own. If she wanted to treat the two deaths as random and unrelated, then she could. And as the executive in charge of her own investigation, she made an executive decision to do exactly that. She would focus only on Nicole's murder. Though the sex thing added another complication.

She tapped the page wondering, not for the first time, who could have hated Nicole enough to want her dead?

The timing hadn't struck her as more than an unhappy coincidence that she'd found Nicole dead the same day they had that ugly and very public fight. Now that she took the first murder out of the equation, she wondered. What if Nicole had been killed that day precisely because she and Toni had the fight?

It was her bad luck and the killer's good luck that she'd even been the one to find the body.

So, if she was right, whoever killed Nicole had seen the fight. Or heard about it, which meant every person at the convention and her hairdresser.

And at the mystery convention? Could Mandeville, for instance, have heard about the makeup slinging match?

She had to admit it was possible.

By the next day she knew that word had somehow got out that she was the person who had discovered Nicole's body. Reporters sought her out, leaving messages on her room's answering service and even trying to track her down in person.

Joseph Mandeville called her room. Not, as it turned out, because he was smitten by her hot bod, but because he thought she might like to be interviewed for his next book. "If you play your cards right," he told her, "you might get your own chapter."

Oh, joy.

She could feel the speculation almost like the whispers that seemed to tickle the back of her neck as she walked into workshops and to meals. No one was outwardly accusing her of anything, of course, not even the police, but she didn't like this awful heaviness sitting over her.

It was time for it to stop.

On a hunch, she called Stacy and invited her for coffee. The poor woman dithered and seemed desperate to think of an excuse not to go, but Toni didn't get to be a National Sales Director without being able to close the deal.

Stacy was sitting alone in the sparsely populated coffee shop when Toni joined her that afternoon.

The smell of the lunch buffet still hung in the atmosphere like the echoes of a sound that's ended. A hint of pasta, the memory of the burner fluid for the hot trays, and the lingering scent of fried potato.

Stacy had chosen the same table where she'd joined Nicole for breakfast the day of her death. Toni wondered if she was even aware of her location. The lunch crowd, like the buffet, was gone—the workshops were in full swing by now. Toni needed a coffee to perk up, she'd slept so badly. She suspected the same was true of Stacy who looked even paler than usual.

After hesitating a moment, Toni walked up to her table. "How are you doing?" she asked softly.

Stacy looked up at her and, if possible, paled even more. "I'm fine."

In her newfound commitment to believing nothing that couldn't be proven, Toni put that down as a big lie. The proof was in the colorless cheeks and trembling hands.

"I'm so sorry about Nicole," she said, and, horrifyingly, her voice trembled with emotion.

Stacy seemed just as shocked. "Why are you crying? You didn't even like her."

"She didn't deserve to die like that. No one does."

"I'm going home," Stacy said, which would have seemed like a non sequitur except that Toni could easily fill in the missing thoughts that led from her statement to Stacy's. She didn't want to die like that and so it was safer to head home.

Toni sat across from the woman and said, "I don't think it's some random psycho. I think Nicole was chosen deliberately."

"But why?"

"I'm hoping you can give me some clues. You were part of her team, you knew her well."

The pale blue gaze drifted lower until Stacy was looking at Toni's top button. "The police already asked me. I had to tell them about your fight. I'm sorry."

Toni waved her apology away. "Of course you had to tell them. Don't worry about it. I told them myself."

"You did?"

"I didn't kill her. Which means that fight didn't have anything to do with her murder.

"Something else caused it. And I think it was something to do with Lady Bianca." Toni picked up her fork and began drawing invisible patterns on the tabletop. "I didn't sleep much last night. I was thinking about why Nicole and I started fighting."

Stacy put her hand on her head as though her headache was coming back. "I should get on the road."

"She pressured you into buying stock you didn't want, and I'm guessing you couldn't afford."

The pale blue eyes swam with tears. She leaned forward and whispered, "I'm going to leave Lady Bianca. I can't do this anymore. I can't lie to my husband."

Toni reached over and patted the other woman's hand. "Don't do that, honey. Don't leave. Most of us don't run our businesses the way Nicole did. You shouldn't let one bad sales director put you off the business."

"It's not just that. I'm really not cut out for sales. I didn't know it would be this much work."

Toni nodded. She knew how important attitude was to success and it was clear that Stacy didn't want success in Lady Bianca enough to put the effort in. Fair enough.

"I feel so bad that you put that five thousand dollars on your credit card just so your team would win the top sales in our division."

Stacy fidgeted a little, flicked her hair over her shoulders and suddenly said, "It wasn't only me. Nicole said she got another ten thousand dollar order on top of mine."

Toni nodded, using a trick she'd seen the detectives use. Waiting and letting the witness keep speaking without interruption.

Stacy glanced at Toni and then away again. "She only told

you about the one because she thought you'd run out and get another big order yourself."

"I don't work that way," Toni said softly. "Sometimes people get so caught up in the competition that they lose perspective. I can't believe she pushed another rep into ordering ten grand worth of stuff so she could scoop another diamond ring. It's insane."

"I hope I can put a stop on my order. I really don't want to have to tell my husband that I spent another five thousand dollars we can't afford."

Okay, so the quiet nodding hadn't worked. Sometimes, a girl had to be more direct. "Who came up with the ten grand?"

"I don't know." Stacy jerked to her feet. "Look, I've got to go. I need to check out and get on the road. I've got a long drive home."

"But aren't you going to stay for the gala banquet? Your team still wins the sales division. You've earned your ring, Stacy. You should collect it."

"No. I can't. I want to go home."

"We're all upset right now. Don't make a final decision yet on quitting."

"Okay. I won't." But it was said more to appease than that she had any intention of continuing on. Too bad. Toni thought she'd shown real promise.

"At least have a coffee before you go. Come on, I insist."

The woman nodded and sat down again. They got their coffees and both sipped quietly for a minute, recruiting strength.

"Did Nicole have a boyfriend?"

Stacy choked and snorted coffee up her nose. Her eyes started to water and she grabbed a napkin. "What did you say?"

"Did Nicole have a boyfriend?" Toni repeated.

"I don't know." But her color was heightened and Toni didn't think it was from her recent coughing fit.

"Why is it a secret?"

"It's not. Look, I should really go. I've got to get on the road."

Toni put a hand on her wrist. "This is important, Stacy. You can't protect Nicole. She's already dead. Don't you want to find out who killed her?"

"He would never have killed her. But it's a secret and I promised I'd never tell a soul. She didn't tell me. I saw him coming out of her room." She slapped a hand over her mouth and snapped her mug to the table.

"Here? You saw him coming out of her room here? At the conference?" She thought of Joseph Mandeville. Oh, she'd give him a chapter for his book all right. "Would you recognize him again if you saw him?"

Stacy looked at her like she'd been in the hot sun too long. "What are you talking about? We see him every day. I promised I'd never tell. She didn't want people thinking she was only sleeping with him to get ahead in the company."

Toni couldn't believe it. "Nicole was sleeping with someone in Lady Bianca?"

Stacy shot her a *duh* look and rose to her feet. "I've really got to go."

She'd never seen Nicole with any of the male reps. Then she realized Stacy had mentioned getting ahead in the company and she knew.

"Orin Shellenbach. She was sleeping with Orin Shellenbach."

"I never told you that. Goodbye Toni," Stacy said, gathering her bag. "Enjoy the rest of your conference."

"Yeah. Bye. Drive safely." Her mind was reeling. Of course, now a bunch of things made sense. Like the fact that she and Melody had known about the Diamond Hard Eyebrow Pencil launch before it was announced. And how Orin had known all about the fight she and Nicole had had only hours after it happened. She'd assumed Nicole had gone running to him to tattle, but maybe it came out naturally during pillow talk.

She'd also confided in Orin about the nasty notes.

Surely Mr. Melanoma wouldn't kill Nicole. Why would he? She was a top producer, an asset to the company and, it turned out, his lover.

Unless she'd threatened to go public with their affair. Or to his wife.

She tapped her hands on the tabletop. The manicure she'd had this morning at the salon wasn't bad, a glossy pale pink, but she missed her diamonds.

Killing Nicole to stop her from destroying his marriage, and, knowing how strait-laced Lady Bianca was, probably his career. Not bad, as motives go.

As Stacy hurried away, her conference bag smacking her legs as though to punish her for cutting out so soon, another thought struck Toni. Stacy had been bullied and pushed by Nicole into five thousand dollars of debt she didn't want. She'd obviously been upset, had she been upset enough to kill? Another person with a motive.

She shook her head at her own foolishness. All Stacy had needed to do was cancel the charge before it went through. Nobody was going to kill another person over a five thousand dollar credit card purchase. At least she hoped not.

The notion tugged at her, though. If Nicole was pushing Stacy like that, logic suggested she was doing the same with her other recruits.

The one she knew the best was Melody Feckler so, blowing off yet one more conference session, she tracked her down finally in the main lobby where she and her husband were hand in hand heading toward the exit.

"Melody, can I talk to you for a second?"

"Stacy left. Did you know?"

Toni nodded.

"I thought at least Nicole's team would stay for the banquet." She blinked a little. Even though she'd obviously made full use of every trick known to a makeup rep, it was still obvious she'd done a lot of crying recently. "Nicole would want us all to go on."

"Absolutely." She touched Melody on the shoulder and sensed Thomas squeezing her hand a little tighter.

"I need to get away for a bit. We're playing a little hooky and going to walk across the street to the mall. I need some black hose to wear with my dress at the gala. Why don't you come with us?"

"Oh, I'm sure the two of you want some time alone."

Thomas spoke up. "It would be a pleasure to have you join us."

"Thanks." Once they were outside, she said, "I'm so sorry about Nicole, Melody. I know you two were great friends as well as colleagues."

The woman nodded jerkily. "She was my inspiration, my mentor and my best friend. She believed in me so completely it made it impossible for me to doubt. A truly great lady and an inspiring leader. Who would kill a woman like that? It's so senseless."

"There's a rumor that one of Nicole's reps put in a ten thousand dollar order right before the deadline. Do you know anything about that?"

Melody dug her sunglasses out of her bag and slipped them on. They were oversized movie-star type dark glasses.

"That's not so unusual. A rep who's really working her business is going to keep needing new stock, you know that. You have to invest in your own success."

For a second she sounded so much like Nicole that Toni was taken aback. "Absolutely, it's just that the order was right before deadline, which made me wonder if Nicole was maybe—" she searched for a softer word than forcing and came up with

—"encouraging her sales associates to put in bigger orders than they were comfortable with?"

Melody stopped in her tracks. They were waiting for an endless red light to turn green in order to cross the freeway. She swung around, rigid in every plane of her body. "She's dead, Toni. You destroyed her last day on earth. Why are you trying to dirty her memory?"

She was taken aback at the violence of Melody's tone. "I'm not. I want to find out who killed her."

"She made some calls back home to her sales reps. Somebody came up with a big order. So what? She didn't live long enough even to wear her tiara and collect her diamond ring." Her voice rose and she stopped speaking to swallow. "The only person who really hated her was you. She's dead. Can't you let her rest?" She grabbed a clean, pressed handkerchief from her bag and dabbed under her eyeglasses. Her husband glared at Toni and wrapped an arm around his wife.

The light turned green and they crossed, arms twined around each other like the devoted couple they obviously were. Toni let them go. She turned back, thinking that she'd caused herself more trouble for nothing.

CHAPTER 22

Beauty is only skin deep, but ugly goes clean to the bone

–Dorothy Parker

TONI GAVE up on the mall and instead went back to her room and flipped on her computer to check her email using the hotel's wireless connection.

She skimmed quickly the subject lines to see what was important. Her book club had assigned a new book. It was Heather Watson's turn to pick, which likely meant something high-brow with a miserable ending. Just what she needed. Enough spam to feed every Monty Python fan around the globe, two messages from sales reps who hadn't been able to attend the conference and then as she scrolled the cursor down she felt as though she'd stepped on a high voltage wire and been blasted by an electric shock.

There was a message from Nicole Freedman. For a second

her heart jumped. Nicole wasn't dead after all. Somehow, she'd made a terrible mistake.

Then common sense reasserted itself. Was it an old email she'd somehow missed? No, it was sent only a few hours earlier.

The subject line was *A Suggestion*. Toni stared at it for a good five seconds, the hairs on the back of her neck prickling, and then she clicked open the message.

Please stop nosing around, or you'll be sorry.

That was it. But the few words were enough to make her feel physically ill.

She wanted to run out of her room screaming. But when she started toward the door, she found herself throwing the wishbone-shaped thing over it instead, keeping everyone out.

Because the idea that someone could send her emails that seemed to be from Nicole made her skin crawl with the possibility that they could be right outside her door at this very moment. Knife raised Norman Bates style.

Of course there wouldn't be anyone out there, but she was too scared to listen to her own sense of reason.

Her hand shook as she called Luke on her cell phone.

He picked up immediately and identified himself.

"It's Toni. I got an email."

The tone of her voice must have told him what kind. "Are you in your room?"

"Yes."

"Stay there. I'm on my way up."

"You're in the hotel?"

"Just got here."

She was waiting by the door, her eye practically welded to the peephole, when he arrived in less than two minutes. It took her a few seconds to unlatch all the safety locks and chains, but he didn't comment. His face was grim as he entered.

"You okay?"

"Yeah." *Pants on fire.*

She led him into the room to the desk where her laptop was still open to that message. He read it, frowning. "What have you been doing?"

"You mean the part where it tells me to stop nosing around?"

"Bingo."

"Nothing." His dark eyes didn't even flicker, they stayed on hers until she burst out, "I can't help it. I found Nicole. This is on my mind, so if I happen to bump into anyone who might know something about her or her business, I might bring up the subject and maybe ask them a simple question or two. That's it. I swear."

He took a step closer and grabbed her shoulders. "This is no time to play Nancy Drew. Two women are dead. You saw how they ended up. This killer's not fooling around."

"I thought—"

"Well, don't. This is a police investigation. Let us handle it."

"Everybody knows I found the body. I've had reporters stalking me, sales reps giving me the evil eye, one of Nicole's reps accused me of ruining Nicole's last day. Don't you see? I am involved."

He paced up and down the room, his hand in his pocket jingling change. Finally, he said, "I think you should go home."

She was shocked, scared even, but the idea of going home hadn't crossed her mind. Suddenly her wobbly legs stiffened. "Go home? You think I should run away because somebody tells me to in an anonymous email?"

She sat down in the chair at the desk, then noticed the email glaring right at her so she pushed her laptop around so she couldn't see the screen.

"Yes. I do."

"We've already got women running home scared. I'm a national sales director. I'm supposed to set an example. If I run home we might as well cancel the conference."

"Not a bad idea."

"Well, we're not going to. Lady Bianca started this company from nothing. We've survived wars, economic downturn and ridicule. Lady Bianca reps do not give up when the going gets tough. Is this the eightieth birthday present we want to give our founder? We quit?"

She shook her head.

"The hotel is crawling with extra security hired by the hotel. We're staying in groups and trusting that you'll catch this nutcase."

"Then let us do our job. The crackpot's right, Toni. Stay out of it."

He jingled some more. If she weren't an extremely patient woman, that could really get on her nerves. "We'll put our tech guys on it, but I'm guessing the email will be untraceable."

"I wish they had a punching bag in the workout room. I need to hit something." Her hands were clenching so her newly polished nails dug into her palms.

"You don't go anywhere alone. You hear me?"

"Yes."

"Don't say it like you're pouting. I'm trying to keep you alive."

"I can't go home. You need my deductive powers."

"Do I?"

"I found out who Nicole's boyfriend was."

"Yeah? Who?"

"Orin Shellenbach."

"Pretty good."

Her jaw dropped open. "You already knew?"

"I'm a detective. A paid professional. Amateurs should mind their own business."

She made a hurumphing sound and put her feet up on the desk. "Lestrade is a professional. You don't see him solving much of anything."

His lips twitched. “You’re reading Arthur Conan Doyle now?”

She shrugged. “I got curious. I went to the mystery readers’ book fair this morning and asked Helen Barnes to recommend something.”

“Excellent. Keep your feet up. Read your book. Leave the rest to us. I’m taking your laptop with me, okay?”

“Sure.” She didn’t think she’d be checking email anytime soon.

Oddly enough, she took his advice. She was so freaked out that she thought a few hours hidden away wouldn’t hurt.

Her mama called, as she’d been doing every few hours. “Are you okay, honey?”

“Yeah, Mama. I’m fine.” She could hear *Better Get to Livin’* playing in the background. She wanted, quite suddenly, to be curled up on her mama’s couch listening to Dolly and drinking coffee. But she put up a good front, and they chatted over all the extraordinary details of Nicole’s murder. “You be careful, Toni.”

“I will, Mama. How’s Tiff?”

“She’s out with some girls she met here in the park. The granddaughters of a neighbor. Nice girls. They went to the mall.”

“Say hi from me. I’ll see you soon.”

For the rest of the afternoon, she napped and read. She needed the peace and quiet. Besides, she was developing a crush on Sherlock Holmes.

Feeling a whole lot better, she came down to the banquet dinner ready to make the most of her remaining time at the conference.

She had the creepiest feeling she was being watched. It was ridiculous. In a crowd of two thousand, of course someone was watching her. Probably several someones. Idly or on purpose. She’d be in people’s line of vision. It happened, exactly as she was now seeing an African American woman who looked stunning in the new cocoa berry lip gloss.

However, the back of her neck kept prickling with unease and, even as she'd turn behind her to check, all she could see were Lady Bianca reps. No one who looked as though they didn't belong.

That was the trouble, of course. She had to face the fact that somehow Lady Bianca was involved in murder. And now, thanks to her nosy ways and extraordinary bad luck of being in the wrong bathroom at the wrong time, the killer's attention seemed to have turned to her.

She needed to figure out what she was going to do about that.

She could take Luke's advice and leave, as plenty of Lady Bianca reps were doing. Pack her bags and head home, hoping the madness would stop and the killer would be caught. But Toni had never been the kind of woman who ran from trouble, and the idea of slinking home in fear from someone who sent anonymous nasty notes was just wrong. She knew the person behind the notes was a vicious killer, but there was something so cowardly about the warning that she thought she might be better to stay and show she wasn't scared than run away in terror. Besides, if she went home and the killer followed her, then she was bringing trouble on her daughter and her mother, and that she wouldn't do.

So, she had to figure out who was trying to scare her and possibly planning to kill her. Preferably long before they struck.

According to Ruth, a dozen delegates went home that day. They didn't know Toni had received a threatening email. It didn't matter. They knew that two women had been murdered in the space of a week and one of them was a Lady Bianca rep. The words serial killer were whispered behind manicured hands.

The whole situation made Toni's blood boil. This was their

big event of the year, when they celebrated beauty and sisterhood and sales excellence. Not when they cowered in fear or cut out early. It simply wasn't right.

She was sharing a round banquet table with her own girls and what was left of Nicole's. She'd been surprised when Melody deliberately chose to sit with her group, but she was so gushingly friendly that Toni understood she was trying to apologize for snapping her head off earlier. She was more than happy to be just as friendly right back.

Other than Melody in manic mode, the table was pretty lifeless. She glanced around the room and saw a similar lethargy.

Orin Shellenbach wasn't the MC tonight. In fact, she didn't think he was present at all. Crying over his dead girlfriend? Or in police custody?

The MC's job had been taken over by another VP, an able administrator with as much personality as a pound of tripe.

"This is just ridiculous," Toni suddenly said. "We've got to stop this dark cloud from ruining our conference. I for one am staying to the end of this conference and I am going to get something out of it."

"Good for you," gushed Melody. She blinked a few times. "In spite of my great loss, I'm planning to stay and get some good information also."

"Excellent. What say we share some beauty tips? That's always fun. I'll start." She thought for a minute. "Okay, this isn't mine, it's my mother's idea, but I thought it was a real good one. Mama found some invitations in the shape of lips and sent them out to all her local customers inviting them to a *Love Your Lips* event, focusing on all our lip products."

Smartphones and notebooks started coming out and already the energy at their table was rising.

"Okay, I've got one," Ruth said. "I sponsored a female bodybuilder who was competing in my town. Think about it. It's not only makeup, there's the body lotions, the body makeup, as well as the full facial products that you can showcase. I ended up getting a lot of publicity from that. I'm going to do it again next year."

And they were off.

If their evening never hit the dizzy heights of perfect happiness, at least Toni knew they'd made something of their time together. And given the killer a symbolic swift kick in the backside.

HER MOTHER'S voice on her cell phone that night made her homesick. And she hadn't lived with her mother for years. That's when she realized how stressed she was.

"Honey? I wanted to hear your voice again. And say good night." Trust a mother, no matter how long it had been since they'd lived together, to know when something was off.

"Thanks, Mama. How are you guys doing?"

"Fine. Tiffany bought me a present at the mall today. A new CD."

Toni's heart sank, thinking of Iron Maiden and Nirvana. "What was it?"

"An album by a young woman named Feist. I'd never heard of her before, but you know she's got a good voice. Maybe a little break from Dolly once in a while is all right, as Tiffany says."

Toni's smile bloomed. "Mama, that's fabulous. Hey, we shared some original marketing ideas, and I told our table about your event. A lot of women took notes."

"That's great. Our *Love your Lips* party was a big success. Tiffany's a natural born saleswoman. It's in the genes, I guess. We sold out of the new fall lip colors completely and in total I guess we did about fifteen hundred dollars worth of business."

"Fantastic!"

"Well, my friends are mostly like me. We go through a lot of makeup. Now if Lady Bianca would only start selling hair spray."

She laughed. "I'll mention it again." Normally, she'd drop a word in Orin's ear, but not this time.

"How's Tiffany doing?" She talked to her daughter every day, but it was nice to get a grandma's eye view.

"She's fine. A little bored, but I'm teaching her to knit. She needs to pick up a few things at the house, though, so we're driving into town. Do you want me to bring you anything?"

"Oh. It's been so crazy around here. I meant to buy some new shoes to go with my dress, but I haven't had a chance." Murder investigations could really cut into a girl's mall time. "Could you bring me my silver heels? Not the ones with the diamond drops all over them, but the ones with the see-through heel? Tiffany will know."

"Sure thing, honey. We'll drop them by tomorrow."

"Thanks, Mama."

And that was one less thing she had to worry about. Not that which shoes to wear to the awards banquet and ball was her biggest priority. Staying alive for it seemed to be.

CHAPTER 23

It sometimes happens that a woman is handsomer at twenty-nine than she was ten years before.

–Jane Austen

HER MESSAGE LIGHT was blinking when she returned to her room after breakfast to brush her teeth before the morning sessions. There was a package at the front desk. Excellent. Her mom must have decided to bring the shoes by early.

When she got to the front desk, a young woman who looked suspiciously like she was chewing on something and trying not to let it show, greeted her.

"Hi. You've got a package for me. I'm Toni Diamond."

The woman swallowed hastily and checked the computer log, then disappeared through the doorway and returned with a corrugated cardboard shipping box about the size of a shoebox, which she handed to Toni.

"Thanks."

Instinctively, Toni reached out and took the box. Then stood there, willing herself not to scream, throw it as far as she could, and duck.

She knew as well as she knew her own Zodiac sign that this box was not from her mother.

The printed shipping label contained her name and the hotel's name on it, but no return address. And the box was wrapped in brown paper. Her mama would have put a heart sticker with a cheery note or something, never have bothered printing out a label, and why would she wrap a pair of Toni's shoes up in brown paper? And not stop to have coffee with her daughter?

Maybe Toni wasn't always the smartest girl on the block, but she tried not to be the dumbest, either. The cardboard box wasn't ticking, but a killer who sent threatening emails might well escalate the threat.

Get rid of it, her brain screamed. *And stop trembling,* she tried to tell her quaking hands.

"You okay?" the girl behind the front desk asked her.

"I'm going outside for some fresh air," she said.

Terrified she'd stumble and blow up half of the hotel, she walked slowly outside holding the box as carefully as though it contained, say, a bomb.

Once outside, Toni crept a few steps away from the hotel entrance then, knowing she couldn't go any further, knelt slowly and gingerly placed the box on the pavement. She watched it for a moment the way she'd watch a deadly snake, hoping that if she stood very, very still, it wouldn't strike. After about ten seconds of non-explosive activity, Toni took a few more steps back and called Luke on her cell.

Luckily he answered right away. "Marciano."

"It's Toni."

"I can't hear you. Why are you whispering?"

"I got an anonymous package. A box."

"Don't open it," he shouted.

Rolling her eyes used up a tad of the nervous energy coursing through her body. "I didn't. I'm standing outside the hotel with it."

"Main entrance?"

"Yeah."

"Step away from the box. I mean it, Toni. Way back. Get behind a cement planter or something. I'll be right there."

But of course she couldn't go far without risking that somebody would pick up the box. They kept the grounds so neat at the hotel, there was always somebody coming around with a garbage bag or a broom. Instead, she stood several yards away from a possible bomb while the few people who walked into the hotel glanced at Toni as though she might perform some service that would require a tip.

She smiled and stayed where she was. For the first time in her life, she wished she smoked so she could at least pretend she had a reason—other than the actual one—for standing out there motionless.

Toni had no idea how fast Luke drove, but based on the way the tires squealed as the blue Taurus turned into the hotel entrance, he could make a respectable showing at Daytona. Not that she was complaining.

He left enough room between his car and the box that he wouldn't cause anything unfortunate to happen to it, and then got out and closed the door carefully.

She didn't think she'd ever been so happy to see anyone as she was when he came up to her and dragged her farther away. Her heart was pounding so hard she felt dizzy. "You take threats to my life seriously. I like that in a man."

"You okay?"

"So far."

Henderson got out, looking leaner and hungrier than ever and stood there for a second squinting at the box.

"Bomb squad's on its way," Luke said. "Why don't you wait in your room? I'll call you when it's safe."

The look she sent him must have given him her opinion of that advice.

"At least stand over there." He pointed past the hotel entrance. She obliged, so he was between her and the bomb. Or box of thank you chocolates. Or extra cosmetics one of the reps had left Toni when they checked out. The more she thought about it the more innocent that box appeared. Just because it wasn't from her mother did not mean it was lethal.

Of course, there was no return address label, no indication at all of who had sent it, which was what had spooked her, the second she'd held it in her hands and looked at it. That, and a slight rattle.

Frank Henderson went into the hotel and stood just inside, presumably to stop anyone who wanted to walk out the front door, though the lobby was thankfully pretty empty.

The bomb squad arrived very impressively only a couple of minutes later, a regular fire truck right behind it. Two guys jumped out of the truck in suits so protected they looked ready to do a moonwalk.

Luke took her arm and led her to the bomb squad truck. The back was already open and one of the guys was taking out a portable X-ray device. "Get inside," Luke ordered.

He walked out to the front of the hotel's drive-through to stop traffic and Toni climbed into the back of the truck, which was mostly a narrow hallway with white metal cabinets on either side. There was a fire extinguisher hanging near the door and the sight of the bright red canister made Toni shudder at the possibilities.

It didn't take long for the bomb squad guys to return. They got into the truck too and using a laptop, were able to see into the box.

Toni maneuvered herself so she could see over the

computer operator's shoulder and nobody stopped her. The image on the screen looked a bit like that of a bag going through airport security. It was all gray and black shapes until her vision adjusted and she could see an outline of what was in the box.

Not that she knew what a bomb looked like, but this didn't appear to be an explosive device.

Still, she shuddered. The box didn't contain extra cosmetics, chocolates or shoes. The contents of the package looked like a mini-coffin with a mini body inside.

The guy manning the laptop hit a few buttons and then said, "There's no explosive material in there, ma'am. Looks like someone sent you a doll."

"Okay," she said, her voice uncomfortably high. "Thanks. Sorry for the false alarm."

"Don't worry about it. A no boom day is a good day."

She smiled dutifully. She couldn't even imagine the kind of stress a guy like that lived under, but he calmly got out of the truck and went and retrieved his X-ray screen.

He motioned Luke over and Henderson came out to join the party.

"It's safe. Go ahead and open it."

Henderson slipped on a pair of surgical gloves, jogged over and retrieved the box. Even though Toni knew it wasn't going to blow up, she still suffered a moment's suspended breath when he bent to pick up the box. But he brought it over without any problem. "You mind if we open it?" he asked her.

"You go ahead."

He eased open the wrapping, like a kid savoring the treat of a birthday present. In this case, she knew he was preserving evidence and swallowed. Inside was a shipping box that you'd get at the post office. He slipped off the lid and revealed the contents.

"Somebody doesn't like you," said Luke.

That was an understatement. Even though she'd seen the X-ray, viewing what was inside that box was still a shock.

The plastic fashion doll sported lots of blonde curly hair. The doll wore the fashion doll equivalent of a business suit in purple, with matching purple plastic pumps. And, in pursuit of a verisimilitude which Toni found particularly cruel, they'd added a chunk of play dough to the doll's nose to make it bigger.

But the most striking feature of the doll was the toy dagger sticking out of her chest; it looked like something from a kid's pirate game. Surrounding the dagger, a starburst of red felt pen spread from the hole in the torso.

"I'll get it straight to forensics," Henderson said.

Luke held onto Toni's arm. She wasn't sure she needed him to, but she was scared to pull away in case she collapsed to the ground.

"Can you grab a ride back with these guys?" he asked Henderson.

The pale eyes glanced from his partner to Toni and he nodded. "No problem."

"Come on," Luke said, pulling her along with him as though he knew her legs might not hold her up much longer.

Toni drew in a lungful of hot Texas air. He opened the passenger door of the unmarked car and she climbed in. As they headed out onto the highway, she asked, "That was from the murderer, wasn't it?" Of course it was a stupid question, but she needed to say the words. And hear the answer.

"Probably. Yeah."

"Nobody's ever hated me that way before." She loathed the way her voice trembled, so she swallowed and tried again. "I've had people mad at me, like Nicole was that last day— But this —" She couldn't finish. Everything she wanted to say sounded melodramatic and contained the word evil.

But it was evil. She'd been murdered in effigy.

She stared at the dusty plastic dashboard in front of her. There was a smell of stale coffee in the car, but the vehicle was neat enough.

"We're going to get that bastard," he said with a suppressed savagery.

"This was different from the note. Doing that to the doll was so vicious." Toni tugged the seatbelt to give herself room to breathe. It was tight as though it had permanently formed itself around Henderson's emaciated frame and was now too lazy to give any extra slack. "I can't believe they did that thing with my nose." She touched the feature in question with her fingertip, as though he might doubt to which nose she was referring. "That was beyond cruel, picking on my worst feature like that. I would have figured that was supposed to be me, without the big nose."

He glanced at her sideways. "I like your nose."

"No one could like this nose." Even her mama had settled for 'your nose has character.' As she'd liked to retort, so did Pinocchio.

"I do. It's a take-no-crap kind of nose. Larger than life. Like you."

She was sure he was lying through his teeth in order to take her mind off the fact that some psycho had made a Voodoo fashion doll in her image and then stabbed it to death, but Toni felt ridiculously complimented.

When she turned to look out the passenger window so he wouldn't see her smile, she realized she had no idea where they were going.

"Where are you taking me?"

"I want you away from the hotel for a while. It's not safe. I plan to bully you into getting out of here and going home and I can't concentrate if I'm worried you'll be attacked."

CHAPTER 24

Strictly speaking, there are no real substitutes for sexual satisfaction.

–Dashiell Hammett

"Can I make a request?"

He glanced at her, looking wary. "Sure."

"I really need a drink. Somewhere with people, but anonymous, you know?" What she most needed was all the stuff that goes with a drink. Social interaction, a convivial atmosphere, feeling anonymous.

"I think I can find someplace."

"Okay then."

They pulled up at a small Italian restaurant, the kind every big city has, where it's almost a secret among locals to keep the tourists out.

The place was busy and noisy but not loud, in the way the best restaurants are. She felt better the second they walked in.

The smell of garlic and rich tomato sauce was comforting and the atmosphere was relaxed, intimate. Even better, there was not a Lady Bianca rep in sight.

Adjoining it was a bar, a cozy area of tiny tables and stools against the granite slab.

"This okay?"

"Perfect." He led her to a quiet corner and they sat down. The table was so small their knees bumped and they quickly rearranged themselves.

"What'll you have to drink?"

"Truth is I'm a lightweight drinker. Normally I'd order a glass of wine, but I've been stabbed to death in effigy. More than overripe grape juice seems required." She glanced up at the blackboard where the drink specials were listed. "A martini, please."

"Gin or vodka?" he asked, thereby slicing through her patina of sophistication faster than the booze would sluice through Toni.

"I have no idea."

He seemed amused by her. And not for the first time. "Never had a martini before?"

"Not that I can remember."

"Okay."

He came back with two. They looked lovely, clear and cool and coma-inducing. Liquid Valium. Exactly what she was going for. "I got one of each. You can decide which you like better."

"Cool. Thanks." Toni sipped the first one. It tasted like iced poison.

She reached for the second. Sipped that. It tasted like iced poison.

"Well?"

"Which one's the vodka?"

"That one."

"Okay. I'll have the vodka."

"Like it?"

"Delicious." She sipped her liquid Valium thinking next time she'd swallow the pill.

"You're a bad liar."

"And a cheap drunk."

"I'm going to get us a table for dinner. The food here's great, and you don't want to be back at the hotel right now."

"That is true."

After a few more sips her martini tasted less poisonous and its medicinal qualities were kicking in. She settled back and started to think how weird this was having dinner alone with Luke without ever having been asked.

"So, you don't have like a doctor-patient thing?"

He looked at her like she might be an olive short of a complete martini.

"I mean, you're allowed to fraternize with..." She had no idea how she would term herself in relation to his world. The best she could come up with was, "civilians involved in your investigations?"

He'd appeared relaxed, leaning back in his chair, but she sensed he'd never totally relax when he was out. Especially if he was with someone who'd been threatened in a rather creepy Voodoo Barbie way. "Is that what we're doing? Fraternizing?"

His eyes were so dark. He wasn't good looking exactly but the man had animal magnetism enough to attract every other animal for miles. He was certainly attracting her.

She sipped again. It was like drinking an icicle, sharp and cold going down.

"Are you seeing anyone?" Not that they were declaring undying love, but she liked to know about a man's romantic status before she got romantic with him.

"Not at the moment. You?"

She smiled as she replied. "Not at the moment."

"Good."

"Good."

And that was pretty much all they said. Somehow, it was all that needed to be said.

Dinner was fantastic, not only because the food was truly good but because Toni wasn't at a table of ten women in a banquet room of a couple of thousand eating the kind of food that gets served to banquets of two thousand people. She didn't have to listen to a motivational, informational or inspirational speaker. In fact, in spite of the truly freaky doll thing, just being out of the hotel was like taking a little break from the bad stuff.

Toni ate ravioli that had pumpkin and some kind of cheese in it, a salad that tasted fresh, and Luke ordered some wine. Italian, of course.

They talked like normal people, about normal things. They didn't talk about the case, until the end of dinner when she said, "I can't believe it. I've been with you for several hours and you haven't bullied me to go home."

"Would you go?"

"No."

"Then I'll save my energy to catch that sick freak."

When they returned to the hotel he didn't drop Toni off out front but drove into the parking garage.

"Are you going to check my room for monsters again?"

He hooked his hand underneath her hair and rubbed her neck in a way that was both soothing and arousing. "Yes."

She reached for her wallet and pulled out one of the two key cards the hotel had given her on check in. "Here. It's still early. I don't want the gossip. Give me five minutes."

Then she got out of the car and headed for the hotel entrance. By skirting the convention floor completely, Toni was able to get to her room without having to make small talk. And if anyone else had been murdered, she didn't want to know.

Once in her room, she slipped off her jacket, then headed for the bathroom and brushed her teeth. She pushed some of her jars and bottles to the side in case he needed counter space for anything.

She fixed the lighting so one bedside lamp cast a nice glow over the bed. A few minutes later, the second key card slid home, and the door opened.

"It's dark in here."

"I could turn on another light."

"Don't bother."

He crossed the floor and took Toni's face in his hands, looked into her eyes and then kissed her. Hot, possessive, somehow sweet. She tasted red wine and pasta sauce and hot, hot Italian man.

She curled her arms around his neck, pressing against him. His gun holster bumped her, and she sucked in a breath. Somehow his job was never far from her consciousness.

"Sorry," he muttered, dragging off his jacket and removing the holster. Knowing her daughter was safe at her grandmother's and Luke and she were in the anonymous comfort of a good hotel snapped all her usual restraints.

Plus, there was a primal need raging within her to celebrate the life that someone was trying to snatch away from her.

When he emerged from her bathroom with his teeth newly clean, she practically attacked the man, grabbing at his buttons, greedy to get to his skin.

He didn't seem to mind at all but reciprocated with an energy that was as flattering as it was arousing.

"You know they say, 'now it's personal?'" she said, mimicking a TV cop. She was snuggled against Detective Marciano.

"Yeah." He turned to kiss her swiftly. "Now it's personal for me, too."

"Whoever is sending these crude warnings is an idiot. They

don't scare me away." Then she paused. "I mean, of course they scare me, but not away. They make me want to stop this psycho, you know?"

"But you are a stubborn and difficult woman," he explained.

"There is that."

"Do you think forensics will find any clues on the doll?"

"You know, you watch too much CSI. Most crimes are still solved by common sense and good detective work. There haven't been fingerprints found on anything, yet. I doubt the doll will yield much of value. Maybe we'll find out where it was bought and when. Maybe we'll get lucky and whoever it was slipped a coupon to the sales clerk for a free Lady Bianca makeover with their name on it."

"But you don't think so."

"No. The killer is psychotic, but smart. Probably watches CSI too."

"You haven't used a gender. Don't you think that using a fashion doll suggests the killer is a woman?"

He shrugged. She felt the movement against her shoulder. "We'll get a profiler and a psychiatrist to study the notes and the doll. When people get fancy like that they reveal a lot about themselves. He or she is getting cocky. Starting to think they're too smart for all of us. That's when they get sloppy. A criminal's arrogance is the detective's friend."

She smiled. "Sounds like a rule."

"Chapter One in the detective's handbook."

"What about Orin Shellenbach? Did he check out?"

"Not as a prize human being, but he's got an alibi for when Nicole was killed. You were there when those four women came into the coffee shop, remember?"

"Yes, of course."

"They stayed chatting until midnight. Shellenbach never left. All four tell the same story."

"Well, I'm glad the killer's not Orin, but I wish we knew who it was."

"Me, too."

"I don't want to talk about this anymore."

TONI WOKE to the smell of brewing coffee.

"That is one of the top three favorite scents in the world," she said to Luke, standing there freshly showered and wearing a white hotel robe.

"Morning, what are the other two?"

"The ocean and," she grinned at him, "your skin, right under your jaw."

He chuckled. "Coffee?"

"Only if you want me to live."

He gestured to the packaged whitener and sugar and she said, "One sugar."

He dumped the package in the coffee, stirred it with a brown plastic stir stick and brought it over to Toni. She sipped her coffee gratefully.

Luke stared at her for a second and suddenly said, in tones of amazement, "They're real."

Toni's eyes widened and she dropped her gaze to her chest. "Of course they're real. What kind of detective are you? I come from a line of well-endowed Southern women."

He shook his head. "I knew those were real. It's your eyes. I thought you wore colored lenses or something."

She laughed. "Honey, it's all real. Well, to be a hundred percent honest, I do sometimes clip in hair extensions and of course, I help my hair color along a little. All makeup does is enhance a woman's natural assets."

"Huh. So you don't wear contacts?"

She shook her head. "Twenty-twenty vision."

"You're full of surprises."

"So are you."

While she sipped her coffee she was thinking.

"Can you check people's bank balances?"

He glanced up. "With a subpoena, sure."

"I think you should check all of Nicole's reps' accounts. Somebody put up ten grand in orders so they would win the division. That's a big order at the best of times, and at the last minute? She had to push them into it."

He nodded.

On his way out the door he kissed her, then held her away from him and gave her his bad cop expression. "You don't go anywhere or do anything without letting me know. Understand?"

She nodded but he wasn't done.

"That doll wasn't for fun. Somebody wants you gone."

CHAPTER 25

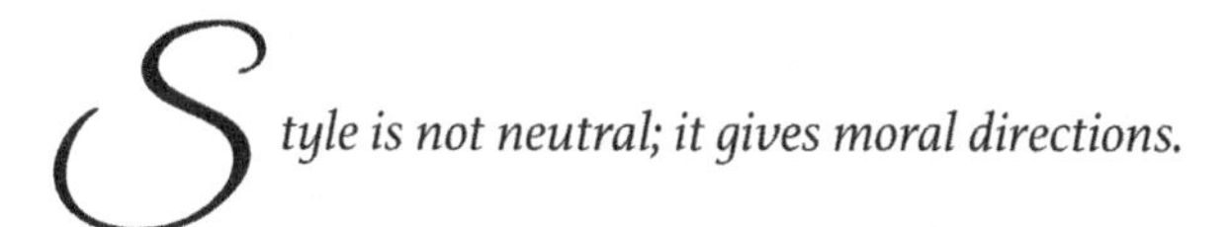

Style is not neutral; it gives moral directions.

–Martin Amis

THE DAY of the awards banquet and gala was always crazy. This year, the energy was indescribable—part manic excitement, part ghost-story fear.

Most of the final day's sessions centered on team building, sales techniques and positive thinking. They ended at noon so everyone had plenty of time to get dressed up, made up and hair styled.

Normally Toni always carried chamomile tea bags, which she'd brew as a calming drink and then run the bags under cold water and place them over her eyes. Nothing worked better for reducing the puffiness. But this trip she'd forgotten tea bags, so she'd gone to her emergency standby and borrowed a couple of stainless steel tea spoons from the hotel which she'd placed in the mini-bar fridge in her room.

She wasn't exactly sleeping like a baby since the trouble had begun and her eyes were telegraphing that fact.

She stripped down to her robe, cleansed her face and applied a Lady Bianca rejuvenating face mask which, in twenty minutes, would cleanse and refresh her skin. In lieu of cucumber slices or chamomile tea bags, she placed the spoons over her eyes when she stretched out on the bed.

Dream images were dancing behind her eyes as she coasted in that twilight state between waking and dreaming.

She sat up with a gasp, her heart pounding and the spoons clattering to her lap, bits of kiwi green rejuvenating mask sticking to them like nuclear reactive pudding.

Everybody lies.

How could you distinguish truth from lies? Fake from genuine? Sometimes you had to be an expert to tell what was true and what was false.

Or get the evidence.

The list of Lady Bianca prize winners for the annual gala would be online by now. She'd be listed, she was certain, for her personal sales volume, even though her team wouldn't win the division.

In fact, every sales rep who had achieved a significant sales volume was listed, with their dollar amount of orders.

She always perused the full list of hundreds of names, all of whom would be recognized at the banquet. She liked to know who was selling as well as she was, whose volumes were higher (not many) and who the up-and-coming stars of the organization were.

She scrambled off the bed and called Suzanne and Ruth's room. Luckily, Suzanne was there and answered.

"It's Toni. I don't have my laptop with me, long story. Are the prize winners up on the website?"

"Mmm-hmmm. And your two favorite ladies are in the prize circle this year," Suzanne said, sounding excited.

"You and Ruth?"

"Yep."

"That's fantastic! Champagne's on me tonight. Listen, I need to borrow your laptop for an hour or so. Is that okay?"

"Sure. I can borrow Ruth's if I need one."

"Thanks, doll. I'm coming right over."

She was halfway out the door when she caught a glimpse of herself and shrieked. Probably better to wash off the green mask before appearing in public.

Five minutes later, cleansed and newly moisturized, she hit the stairs, ran down a flight and knocked on Ruth and Suzanne's door. Ruth's face was kiwi green, Suzanne's was French-clay white. They hugged carefully, and she sped back upstairs with Suzanne's laptop under her arm.

"Come on," she said as she waited for the old computer to boot up. Now that Suzanne was making so much money, maybe she could spring for a new laptop.

At last. She logged onto the Lady Bianca website and used her password to get to the restricted part of the site for reps only.

She scanned the list quickly, found her name, and then Suzanne's and Ruth's.

More significantly, every single rep on Nicole's team was in the upper sales level. Every. Single. One.

The awards were based on how much wholesale product a rep purchased from the company. The idea was that the product would end up sold retail, but the rep would still be recognized even if the product sat in a garage gathering dust.

"Wow, I was right," she said aloud as she grabbed her cell and called Luke.

"Hey," he said when he heard her voice, his going low and sexy. "How you doing."

"I'm okay. Listen. Can you come upstairs? There's something you've got to see."

"You sound serious. Does that mean it's not you, naked?"

"Not this time."

"On my way."

"SEE WHAT I MEAN?" she said when Luke sat beside her on the bed, the laptop on his knees. "I think you should look at Melody Feckler's bank accounts and credit cards. Look at that sales volume. There is no way she is selling that much product. I'm sure she's the one who pledged ten grand to Nicole the day she was killed."

"And then popped her best friend?"

"I'm positive she's lying about how well she's doing. That's all. A couple of things aren't adding up. Her clothes are cheap." He gave her a funny look. "I mean, inexpensive. She always shares a room, except this time because she got it for nothing because her husband works for the hotel chain. And she's the only one who would make that kind of commitment to Nicole on the spur of the moment."

He patted her on the back. "Good work. I gotta go but I'll see you tonight. At the banquet." He traced his fingertip along her hairline. "But you might want to wash the green slime out of your hair first."

She opened her eyes wide. "You're coming to the banquet?"

"Wouldn't miss it."

"Are you bringing me a corsage?"

He kissed her. "Don't push your luck." And he was gone.

CHAPTER 26

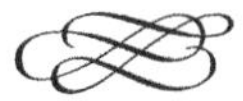

Love of beauty is Taste. The creation of beauty is Art.

–Ralph Waldo Emerson

THE PHONE RANG as Toni was securing the last hot roller. "Honey, it's me."

"Mama." She juggled the phone around a stubborn roller. "Hi. What's up?"

"I'm downstairs with your shoes."

In the craziness she'd completely forgotten the shoes. "You're here? Now?"

"We have a surprise for you. Tiffany and I are staying over tonight at the hotel. We got tickets for the gala." She lowered her voice. "In fact, there were lots of cancellations so tickets and a room weren't a problem. They were even able to put us on your floor."

"Fantastic. Come on up."

But it wasn't fantastic. She loved her mother and daughter too much to want them to be here where two murders had occurred. She took a deep breath. Only a few more hours of the conference remained. What could go wrong? The hotel was packed with police, extra security guards hired by Lady Bianca and a couple thousand sales reps. Toni didn't plan to let her daughter or her mama out of her sight. So long as they stayed together they'd be fine.

She opened the door to her two favorite women in the world, hugging them both.

"Mama, you lightened your hair." *Again.*

Linda twirled and struck a model pose. "Platinum is the new blonde."

"And old is the new young," Tiffany mumbled behind her so only she could hear.

"Tiff and I put our things in our room, but I wanted to bring you your shoes."

"The ones with the see through heels, right?"

"Tiffany knew which ones they were."

"The 'Cinderella is a ho' slippers."

She bumped her unruly offspring with a hip. "Those are the ones. One day, Goth will be a thing of the past and I will be able to throw at you all the one-liners I've been saving up."

Tiffany snorted. "I can't wait."

"Goth is the new black," she said, backing into the room and putting the shoes on the bed.

"Goth is never having to say you're happy."

"Goth to a flame," Linda added.

Toni laughed. "Good one." Even Tiffany was grinning.

"I have to go down early, but I'll stop by on my way." She wrinkled her nose. "Do you have a dress, Tiffany?" Last time she'd looked, her daughter's closet contained nothing but black jeans, shirts and sweaters, all either secondhand or made of renewable resources like hemp or bamboo. No doubt with cruelty-free cutting practices so the bamboo didn't feel any pain.

"I lent her one of my gowns," Linda said.

Toni couldn't even imagine.

"Don't worry," her mama said brightly. "Tiffany managed to make it work for her."

When she walked to her mother and daughter's room forty minutes later, with her hair curling around her shoulders, her cosmetics perfectly applied and her dress on, she wondered what she'd find inside.

Tiffany was lounging on one of the queen-sized beds. Her makeup was her usual black and white, but she'd toned down the drama, at least, and had slicked on some colored lip gloss. As Linda said, she'd made one of her grandmother's dresses work for her. The plain black, figure-hugging dress with its plunging neckline was eye-popping when her mother wore it.

Tiffany had slipped a white T-shirt underneath it and since she was much taller than her grandmother, the dress stopped above her ankles. With black leather lace-up boots, a peace symbol on a leather cord necklace and her black nose stud, she had indeed made the dress her own.

She was all ready to go, and using the interval before the banquet started to read a book called *Our Final Hour: A Scientist's Warning: How Terror, Error, and Environmental Disaster Threaten Humankind's Future In This Century—On Earth and Beyond.*

"Oh, honey, you look wonderful," Linda said, emerging from the washroom.

She regarded her reflection in the long mirror on the wall. The light cast back the glitter of silver from her gown. This was an important banquet and everyone was encouraged to dress up, but even for Toni the gown was a little flashy. In the store, it hadn't seemed so—sparkly—as it did now, and she'd loved the profusion of diamonds across the low-cut bodice. "Is this too much?" Toni asked.

Tiffany looked up from her book. "Are the oceans polluted? Is global warming destroying the planet as we know it?"

"Don't get above your raising, Tiff," Linda Plotnik warned, shaking a finger at her mouthy granddaughter. To Toni she said, "Of course it's not too much. You look dazzling."

"Pot, meet kettle," Tiffany said and went back to her book.

"You should be proud to have such a gorgeous mother."

"Grandma, haven't you ever heard that less is more?"

"Not in my world, honey. When you've been as poor as your mom and I have, you know that more is more."

"Oh, shoot," Toni said. Clapping a hand to her hair. "That reminds me. I forgot my tiara. I've got to go back and get it. Well, wish me luck. I'll see you after the presentations. Save me a seat for dinner?"

"You bet, honey. We're so proud of you."

"You rock, Mom."

She was smiling as she emerged into the corridor and headed toward her room.

She stopped with a gasp.

A man in a hotel uniform was coming out of her room, closing the door behind him.

"Excuse me? Can I help you?"

The man turned, and she recognized him.

"Thomas Feckler? What were you doing in my room?"

"Dropping off your suicide note."

CHAPTER 27

I live by a man's code, designed to fit a man's world, yet at the same time I never forget that a woman's first job is to choose the right shade of lipstick.

–Carole Lombard

"SUICIDE NOTE? Are you out of your mind?" Then she saw the knife in his hand, long and wicked, and when she looked into his eyes, she saw the answer to her second question.

She turned and ran, not for the room where her daughter and mother were, instinct screamed, but for the exit door to the stairs, cursing her tottering heels. She didn't get far before he grabbed her arm. His fingers had a surgical glove covering them, but even through the latex, she could feel how hot his hands were.

"I don't think you should run. Or scream. What if your mother or your daughter comes out to see what is going on?"

Her heart hammered, and she stopped dead. How could he

have known? But, of course, he worked for the hotel chain. Which was how he'd so easily found his way into her room. "They have nothing to do with this."

"And why don't we keep it that way, hmm?"

She nodded. Licking her lips and tasting the raspberry flavor in the lipstick.

He twisted her arm behind her back and pushed the tip of that monstrous knife against her lower back. "Now, we walk. If we pass anyone, you act normal."

She snorted. "Or what? You'll kill me?" Did he think she was stupid? With that knife, he wasn't planning to cook for her.

"Or I'll add your daughter and your mother. Understand?"

She nodded.

"I did everything I could to warn you away. This is your own fault." He brandished the knife at her as though she had any doubt what he meant by "this".

"You mean, my murder." Let him hear that word.

"Nicole wouldn't listen either."

"Do you really think there's any way you'll get away with a third murder?"

He shook his head, giving her a little, knowing smile that gave her the creeps. "You're not going to be murdered. You'll commit suicide."

"Suicide?"

"Mmm. It's very sad. You and Nicole had that huge fight, everybody saw you. Then you killed her. You even discovered the body and, as everybody knows, half the time it's the murderer themselves who pretends to discover the body."

"But why—"

"Guilt of course. You can't live with yourself any longer. How appropriate that you're going to throw yourself on this knife."

She stared at the thing in horror. Its blade was particularly shiny, even in the dim light of the hallway. And very long.

A weird sound came out of her mouth. One she wasn't proud of.

"Oh, don't worry. It's not the same knife that killed Nicole. You needed something longer. A sword would be better—very Roman—but you'll manage with the industrial carving knife."

She felt sick. Bile was rising into the back of her throat. She swallowed it down.

She thought of her mother and daughter only a couple of doors away, who would be emerging very soon. She couldn't let them run into this madman.

She walked along with him as quickly as she could. They passed the elevators and she couldn't figure out their destination.

Thomas Feckler? Thomas Feckler a murderer? It didn't make sense. "But Melody. How could you do that to Melody? Nicole was her friend."

"I love my wife." If he'd ever spoken a truth, she knew that was it. There was a ring of sincerity in the words. "I'd do anything for Mel. Anything. I'd die for her."

"Even kill for her?"

"To protect her. Only to protect her. That woman," he spat out the words, "with her smarmy ways, 'I love you so much, I know you can be a star' all she wanted was her own success. She didn't care about Melody. But Mel fell for the line. She kept buying more and more product. At first I supported her. She was so happy and excited about her new business. But her sales weren't keeping up with her overhead. I tried to explain but she wouldn't listen. She'd fallen under her spell. She was like one of those princesses in the fairy tales who are enchanted by an evil witch." No question who the evil witch was in his story.

"I finally sat her down one day and told her we were in danger of losing the house, but she kept telling me I had to have faith in her and believe in her and her business. It was making me crazy."

No kidding.

"Then I overheard her on the phone with Nicole—they used to talk all the time on the phone—she didn't know I was home. It was obvious from her end of the conversation that Nicole was describing ways to get money without me finding out. After that I started reading all her emails and—"

"But that's like reading someone's mail. It's private," she burst out without thinking.

He jabbed the knife, not hard, but enough that she felt the fabric of her dress tear and the sharp blade against her side. "Nothing should be private between a man and his wife."

"So, Melody knows about how you've killed her mentor?"

He looked highly insulted. "That's different. I have to protect my wife. Besides, Nicole kept saying she should divorce me if I wasn't supportive. That woman was evil. I had to stop her."

"And stop Melody from spending all the family money and leaving you." Toni had no idea why she couldn't put a cork in it, but nerves and panic seemed to have an unfortunate effect on her mouth.

"Once Nicole's influence was removed, I knew Melody would see reason." The Melody she'd seen recently, who spouted Nicole's lines like a recorded message didn't seem any different than she'd always been, but by dint of biting her tongue, Toni managed not to blurt out that observation.

"The ten thousand was the last straw, wasn't it?"

He nodded briefly.

"Did Nicole help Melody get a company credit card too?"

He snorted. "She already has one of those. No, she went to bat for Melody so she could have her limit raised by another ten grand."

"My God."

"Exactly." He shook his head and his perfectly cut hair fell back into precise order. "I am not a violent man, but we're going to lose our house. I've spent years at the hotel, working my way up. I could be a hotel manager one day. But not if I go bankrupt." He stopped to drag in air, he sounded breathless, as though he'd been sprinting. "I can't lose it all. You should see our garage, it's so full of makeup and creams and promo items you can't even move. Haven't parked a car in there in two years. Nicole talked her into buying thousands of sampler packs last year and then they changed the colors. Boxes of those things." He was getting seriously worked up. Beads of sweat dotted his hairline and his voice was rising. She could feel the tremble go all the way through the knife.

"You planted one of those old sampler packs on Amy Neuman's body." Nicole hadn't lied after all. She'd never given the woman a sampler pack. If only she'd made a bigger deal about that sampler pack at the time. If only.

"I thought she was Nicole Freedman. I wanted Nicole to choke on those sample packs; tossing one at her while she was dying was the closest I could get."

"Oh, my God. You mean, Amy died because of mistaken identity?"

"A terrible mistake. I found a time when no one was at the front desk, checked the computers and found Nicole's room number. I was watching the door when that woman came out of Nicole's room."

"You didn't check for ID before stabbing her?"

He ignored her. She felt a wetness at her side. No pain, though. Probably she was in shock. "Nicole and I had never been introduced, but she'd been telling Melody for some time that she wanted to meet me and explain how important it was that I support Melody's success." He laughed in a creepy, humorless way. "This woman who'd been encouraging my wife to go behind my back, to divorce me.

"She didn't pay any attention to the emails warning her away. So, I decided, we'd meet. And I brought along one of those old sampler packs to tell her what I thought of her and her sales techniques."

She thought back to the morning that Amy Neuman had been discovered stabbed to death. "But you weren't even here that night."

Again with the creepy smile. "I was. It's a four-hour drive to our house from here. I drove in, planned to meet with Nicole, convince her to stop ruining our lives, and drive home again. Then, things went wrong—"

"But you must have realized that wasn't Nicole."

He shook his head. "I thought she was just blowing me off. She kept saying, 'I don't know what you're talking about,' but she was shaky and angry, so I figured she was lying."

"Except that she really didn't know what you were talking about. All she had was a makeover."

Thomas Feckler sighed. "I regret her death. Very much. But, since you've admitted to the murder and will be punished, I'm sure I'll one day get over the pain."

He pulled her into an unobtrusive door that led to the service area and the big cage-like elevator.

"Where are we going?" she asked as he pushed the button to call the elevator.

"The basement."

CHAPTER 28

A man's face is his autobiography. A woman's face is her work of fiction.

–Oscar Wilde

Luke walked into the ballroom and stalled. He'd seen a lot of unusual sights in his time. Murder victims in pieces, the remains of gang turf wars and suicides where the guy's brains were spattered from here to kingdom come. He'd assumed he was immune from shock. Turned out he wasn't.

The ballroom was packed with women and all of them wore Miss America type sashes and pins, jewels and fancy dresses. And the tiaras. There were thousands of tiaras winking in the light from the dripping chandeliers. If this was a country, they'd be all royalty with no subjects.

Even in Bling Kingdom it wasn't difficult to spot Linda Plotnik and her granddaughter.

Linda wore a white gown covered in sequins and sparkling

beads, draping the floor. When she raised her arms, it was like iridescent wings. Long chandelier earrings dangled from her ears and her hair was piled high. Naturally, a tiara nestled in the white-blonde curls.

Tiffany was yin to her yang, black to her white, negative to her positive. She'd taken a black gown and managed to turn it into an ironic statement. Interesting girl, that Tiffany. Among all the updos and tiaras, her hair was hanging too black and too long. Her face was white with black outlined eyes. If anything, all that heavy black makeup had the opposite effect of the one she intended. The heaviness only emphasized the delicacy of her features and her youth. In a few years, she'd be as gorgeous as her mother.

Speaking of which, he glanced around. "Where's Toni?"

Linda pointed to the program. "Right here. She should be out to get her award in about half an hour. Isn't it exciting? Wait till you see her dress."

He'd be excited when the conference was over and everybody went home safe and sound. The fact that tonight was the killer's last chance, and that he or she had it in for Toni, was not making him happy. Of course, there'd been no incidents since the doll, and she'd promised him to leave the sleuthing to the police, so he concentrated on keeping his eyes and ears open, and the police presence obvious.

"I'm going to take a walk. I'll be back before she comes out."

THE SERVICE ELEVATOR caged Toni in with a nightmare. A murderous psycho with a knife who'd told her flat out he planned to kill her.

Think, she ordered herself, but with a madman waving a deadly knife at her—a madman who'd already killed two women—it was impossible to think.

At some point, her mom and Tiffany would notice that she

wasn't there. All they had to do was alert Luke—or any other cop—and the police would start combing the hotel for her. Of course, it would be a while before anybody got around to the basement. A fact she was certain Thomas Feckler had taken into consideration.

The elevator settled to the ground with a bump that made her gasp and he pushed the button that lifted the door. He hauled her out of the elevator at knifepoint and they scuttled out like waltzing crabs.

Thomas Feckler listened but there was no sound. The basement smelled musty. There were no windows down there, and the industrial lighting was dimmed, probably because it was night time and no one was working down here.

Toni knew that if she screamed he'd kill her immediately and if there was no one in the vicinity screaming was clearly pointless. He seemed to have a destination in mind as they walked along a corridor. "Where are we going?"

"I've got a spot all picked out where it's easy for you to fall on your knife. I think everyone at Lady Bianca will be proud of you for ending your tortured life with dignity."

"Why on earth would I make it easy for you?"

The glance he sent Toni was impatient. "If you cooperate, your death will be swift. Like Nicole's. If you don't, I'll carve you into ribbons and leave you to die slowly. Very unpleasant. I started my hotel career working in the kitchens, you know. I'm pretty good with a knife."

LUKE STROLLED out of the massive ballroom and headed for the front lobby. There were security guys from a private firm hired by the hotel and a couple of undercover officers, one dressed as a cleaner the other as a parking attendant.

Everything was quiet. Routine.

He walked back across the marble lobby. Made his way to

the backstage area but it was so crammed full of women that he couldn't squeeze his way through. Toni was in there somewhere, no doubt in a gown that would make his eyes pop out, and a tiara.

He had no idea how he'd fallen for a big-haired, high maintenance, nosy cosmetics saleswoman, but he had. Crazy. But sometimes crazy was good.

Next, he checked the elevators, the restaurant, even glanced in the lobby gift shop. Everything as it should be. Still, he couldn't shake the itch, deep in his gut, that trouble lurked.

The kitchen was staffed to the max, full speed, full efficiency, as they got ready to serve twenty-five hundred dinners.

The grumpy female chef glanced up and nodded when she saw him.

"How are things back here? Any knives missing?"

"Crazy busy. My blades are all here, apart from the one you have in custody," the female chef said. "Oh, and the chef's knife I sent out for sharpening."

The head chef turned to her. "The Misono? Fourteen inch?"

She nodded.

"It came back this morning, before you came on shift. I signed for it." He strode forward to her station. "I put it right there so you wouldn't miss it."

They all looked at the spot he indicated. There was no knife there.

"What time was that?" Luke snapped.

"Around noon, I think."

"What time did you come on shift?"

"Two."

He raised his voice to a bellow. "Okay, listen up everyone. Who came through here between noon and two today?" There were mutters and shrugs and blank looks. He made his voice deliberately rough. "Come on, people. We've got a killer out there armed with one of your knives."

"People come through here all the time," the female chef wailed. "Wait staff, kitchen help, the extra security guys, even a doorman came through here, so great, now we've got murderers in the kitchen."

But Luke was already running back the way he'd come. He hauled out his radio. "Henderson, there's a knife missing from the kitchen." He heard the curse and echoed it in his head. "Check out Toni's room. Killer could be wearing a uniform."

Next, he contacted the undercover cop in the parking garage. Told him to check Toni's vehicle.

Then he pounded to the backstage area of the ballroom. This time he didn't worry about squeezing in. He shoved women out of the way and forced his way into the mob.

Way up front he could see the lit stage, so covered with balloons it was like being underwater in a particularly garish fish tank. Streamers instead of seaweed and row upon row of ball-gowned women.

"Toni Diamond," he shouted. "I'm looking for Toni Diamond."

One smart-aleck tried to shush him and he yelled over her. "Police. Where's Toni Diamond?"

"She's supposed to be beside me, but she's not here yet," a voice finally yelled back.

The itch in his gut turned into a full-scale jackhammer.

His radio crackled to life. "Yeah?"

"I'm in Toni's room. There's a suicide note."

"What does it say?"

The emotionless voice read: "To whom it may concern: I can no longer live with two murders on my conscience so I am taking my own life. Please forgive me. Toni Diamond."

"The killer's got Toni."

He ran back to the ballroom. The awards ceremony continued. They hadn't heard him, he supposed, and he decided it was good that things should continue as normal. If the killer felt undetected they had more time.

He waded through the tables to Linda and Tiffany. "How's it going?" he asked them.

"Fine. I'm glad you made it back. She should be out in ten minutes or so."

"When did you last see her?"

"About twenty minutes ago." Linda's forehead creased. "Is everything all right?"

"Yes. I wanted to wish her luck, is all. Have you seen Melody Feckler?"

"Two tables over and three forward. She goes in the second award group."

"Thanks."

"Is Mom okay?" He couldn't look at that girl with her mother's eyes and her intelligent, serious face and lie.

He walked up to her. "I think she might be in trouble. But I'm going to find her." He grabbed her shoulder and squeezed. "I promise. But you have to keep calm and let me do my job."

She looked at him and nodded.

"Good girl."

He jogged forward to where Melody Feckler had squeezed herself into a pale orange silk number that made her look like an uncooked sausage.

Not a care in the world. And no sign of Toni. He scanned the table. They were all there, except Stacy, who'd gone home early.

And the husband.

"Mrs. Feckler?" He knelt by her side and spoke loudly enough to be heard over the award announcements.

"Yes?"

"Where's your husband?"

She smiled the smile of the innocent. "He's not feeling too

well. I think it was the burritos at lunch. He's lying down." She giggled. "Guess you were looking for some male company?"

He nodded and moved away.

Out in the hall, he radio'd Henderson. "It's Thomas Feckler. And the bastard's got Toni."

"Any idea where he's got her?"

"No."

"We'll start with his room."

"I want every inch of this hotel searched."

CHAPTER 29

An open enemy is better than a false friend.

–Greek proverb

THEY WALKED down the dim hallway together, Toni slightly ahead, her high heels tip-tapping on the cement floor like a society woman. Thomas Feckler, in his neat hotel uniform, could be her doorman or chauffeur.

"Won't Melody wonder where you are?"

"I'm in our room, lying down." He checked his watch. "I'll be back before she knows I've left."

"What about the...mess?" she asked, then wished she hadn't.

"This isn't my uniform. It belongs to the hotel. Underneath it, I've got street clothes. I doubt there will be any mess with you, but I don't want any inconvenient DNA evidence linking us. I'll put the uniform in a laundry bag, slip out the service entrance, throw the bag in a dumpster a few blocks away and return. No one will ever know I was here."

"You've thought of everything," she said, trying to sound admiring while searching crazily for some kind of weapon or help. If she could get him off guard enough to get him to lower the knife, Toni thought she might have a chance. Slim to none. But what choices did she have?

The hallway was lined with laundry carts. They passed a cavernous room filled with industrial washing and drying machines big enough to shampoo and blow dry a horse. All ominously silent, watching with their huge black eyes. Liquid laundry soap in twenty gallon drums sat beside them. They passed a rack of fluffy white robes with the hotel crest on the pockets hanging there like a dance line of ghosts.

Toni's eyes darted around frantically, looking for escape. Help. A weapon. Something. The hallway continued, cinderblock walls, cement floor. The ceiling was open and tracks of electric wiring snaked between sprinkler heads and fluorescent lighting fixtures.

Thomas Feckler walked casually at Toni's side, but she wasn't fooled. The knife was razor sharp and never not pressing into her.

"I didn't think of everything," he snapped. "I didn't think about how thousands of women together would gossip constantly, or that you would turn out to be so interfering and nosy."

"Speaking of nosy, thanks a lot for sticking an extra big nose on my voodoo doll. That was really cruel."

"Oh, come on. You're a beautiful woman. It was Nicole who always used to call you Pinocchio—that's how she referred to you in her emails to Melody. That's where I got the idea."

Toni's jaw dropped. "She called me Pinocchio?"

"Well," he giggled, "she won't be doing that anymore."

Right. And Toni wouldn't be around to care, not without some kind of fight. She'd once taken self-defense for women. It was a long time ago and she couldn't remember much, but there was one weapon she had on her that she recalled from that long-ago class.

Her heels.

Visualizing success with more concentration than she'd ever done in her life, she took a deep breath.

She pretended to stumble onto her left shoe. The heels were so high she almost made the stumble real. It threw them both a little off balance which caused Thomas to tighten his grip on her. Tucked up tight against him, she lifted her right foot and stamped down her spiked Plexiglas heel with all her strength and drove the spike into the top of his foot.

Fear, adrenalin, and fury lent her strength, she grunted with the impact, felt it shudder up her shin bone, then heard the man behind her scream with pain and *Yes!* She heard the knife clatter to the floor.

She turned and kicked the knife down the corridor in the direction they'd come. It slid a nice long way. Probably she should have scrambled for it but she dimly remembered that defense class where the instructors warned that the attacker could too easily turn a woman's weapon against her.

Toni figured her best hope for escape was to find the exit and get the hell out of here.

Thomas Feckler made animal grunts as he stumbled to his feet and hobbled painfully after the knife. Toni ran forward. She'd have liked to stop and slip off her shoes, but she couldn't take the time. Besides, years of practice in heels make her pretty fast. Especially with the fight or flight response blasting through her like jet fuel.

She sprinted forward, passing another big drum of laundry soap. She could hear Thomas Feckler breathing heavily and grunting with each step. He seemed to be going in the other direction, no doubt to retrieve the knife. She hoped she'd broken every bone in his foot.

Of course, when he got that knife he'd come back for her.

He also knew where the exits were and she didn't. She had to slow him down.

Her breath was coming in panting gasps, which echoed so the walls seemed to be in distress.

She turned, wasting precious seconds and ran back to the huge tub of liquid laundry soap, pulled the plug out of the plastic lid and, with a huff of effort, heaved it onto its side, watching the thick liquid glug out onto the cement floor.

She took off again. Rounded another corner. A storage area. More laundry soap and huge buckets of some white powder as well as a wall of cleaning supplies.

She pulled the plug on a second drum of soap and left it overturned and oozing slime onto the floor behind her. One more corner. It was like a maze down here and she'd completely lost any sense of direction.

Grabbing a bright red fire extinguisher off the wall, she followed the next jog in the hallway.

And stumbled onto a mountain of towels. There must have been thousands of white hotel towels heaped beneath a massive laundry chute. Three walls. A dead end but for a closed door on the other side of the towels.

"Please," she whispered as she ran for the door.

It was locked.

"No!" she yelled. She bashed at the door handle with the fire extinguisher but it didn't fly open like in the movies.

She was trapped.

Her gaze darted around the area. Amazingly, she bounced past it twice before she recognized a plain black phone attached to the wall. She leapt for it even as she heard Feckler getting closer.

"Hello? Hello?" she screeched into the phone.

"Housekeeping," a voice said. A real live voice.

"Thank God. This is Toni Diamond. I'm trapped in the basement laundry area. Thomas Feckler has a knife. Tell Detective Marciano. Tell the cops."

"Miss? Where are you?"

"The laundry room. Downstairs in the hotel. Get the cops!" she screamed.

She thought about diving under those towels and burrowing deep inside, the way she might have hidden in her bedclothes back when she was a kid and frightened of monsters. But this was a real life monster and she couldn't stand the thought of cowering under there while he systematically worked his way through the towels until he found her.

Maybe she was going to die, but she was a woman in a sparkling dress and this princess was going to go down fighting.

She pulled the pin on the fire extinguisher as she ran back, pressing herself against the wall. He'd have to pass her. With any luck he'd be past her before he saw her, and her pounding heart wouldn't give her away.

The next few moments were the most terrifying of her life. She stayed pressed against the beige cinderblock wall, the extinguisher heavy in her hands, listening as the wheezing, grunting, muttering Feckler drew closer.

Hitchcock couldn't have filmed anything more frightening than the way his shadow came into view before he did, a colossal figure, brandishing a long, sharp knife.

Then the real Feckler came into view. He was walking carefully through the slick soap, but sadly he hadn't slipped on it and cracked his head. All she'd done was slow him down. He stared at the towels. "I know you're in here," he panted. "There's no way out." He limped forward. "Are you hiding? Shall we play hide and seek?"

She aimed the nozzle of the fire extinguisher and squeezed the handle, letting Feckler have it.

The blast wasn't strong enough to do any damage, but at least it might disorient him enough that she could get back down the corridor, back to the elevator and freedom.

She might even be able to knock him out with the metal canister if she could get close enough to him without being stabbed.

"You are ruining everything," he screamed. She kept the stream of fire retardant spewing into his face. As he lunged at her, she thought he'd let go of whatever sanity he'd clung to. Feckler's howl echoed off the walls as he ran at Toni with the knife raised. The foam had matted his perfect hair and clung to his face so he looked like the loser in a pie throwing contest. She squirted him again as he came at her with that knife in murder mode.

Holding the fire extinguisher in front of her like a shield, she backed toward the corridor.

He was running blind. And he'd forgotten the soap.

Feckler's feet hit the pool of liquid soap and his legs flipped out from under him. She heard the wet smack as the man's body hit the soapy ground.

Any hopes she had that he'd knocked himself out were soon gone.

The mix of rage and bruised vanity that spewed forth from his mouth sounded like another language. Toni turned to run back the way they'd come, but she couldn't move fast or she'd slip too. As she picked her way, Feckler scissored his legs out and tripped her, so she tumbled down to the soapy floor too.

He was rolling around, grabbing for her and he was hanging onto that knife a lot harder than he was holding onto sanity.

At that moment, she heard Luke yell, "Toni?"

"Luke!" she cried. "Down here by the laundry chute." She pulled up to her hands and knees and crawled toward safety. In that second, as she thanked God, her lucky stars, the Corvallis

Police Department, and Detective Luke Marciano, Thomas Feckler grabbed her ankle and yanked.

With a muffled scream, she bounced toward him, but managed to toss herself away from that deadly blade, so her body dropped sideways across Feckler's like something out of WWF.

He grunted when Toni fell on him, breaking her own fall and jabbing him in the solar plexus, but the man was beyond feeling pain. His teeth were bared and even as Toni grabbed the wrist holding the knife, he was flipping over, taking her with him.

She could hear the pounding of feet getting closer. Luke wasn't alone.

She tried desperately to stop Feckler from rolling on top of her but she couldn't get any traction in the pool of liquid soap. It was like they were Jell-O wrestling on a cement floor, except that this bout was in deadly earnest.

"Luke," she yelled as loud as she could. "Here!"

Feckler grabbed her skirt and yanked Toni forward. She kicked at him with all her might, but all she did was slide. She was tiring fast, her arm trembling with the effort of holding off that knife.

Feckler bared his teeth and shoved, rolling over until he was on top of Toni, the knife poised above her throat where she could feel her pulse jangling.

She heard the stomp of feet and the abrupt stop of same. But she couldn't see anything. Nothing but Thomas Feckler's face, feral and mad above her.

"Drop the knife and back away," Luke ordered in a calm, commanding voice.

She and Feckler were both slippery and sticky with soap. Her eyes burned and her lashes felt gooey.

"If I'm going down, I'm taking this nosy woman with me," Feckler snarled. He raised the knife and Toni knew this was it.

She wasn't sure whether it was a memory from self-defense for women or instinct, but she heaved her knee up between Feckler's legs with all the strength she could muster. It wasn't much, but the impact was enough to make her attacker jerk his head back in pain.

"Aagh," he said.

Followed immediately by the blast of a bullet. Feckler's body jerked and blood rained down on Toni. She rolled her body to the side so that the knife clanked harmlessly to the cement.

She was smothering. She heard the grunts of effort coming from her throat as she heaved and pushed to get the body off.

Luke was there, rolling Feckler away. He kicked the knife to the side and dragged Toni to her feet.

"Don't look," he ordered, but it was too late. She'd already seen Feckler. Half his head had blown off.

CHAPTER 30

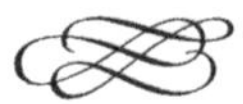

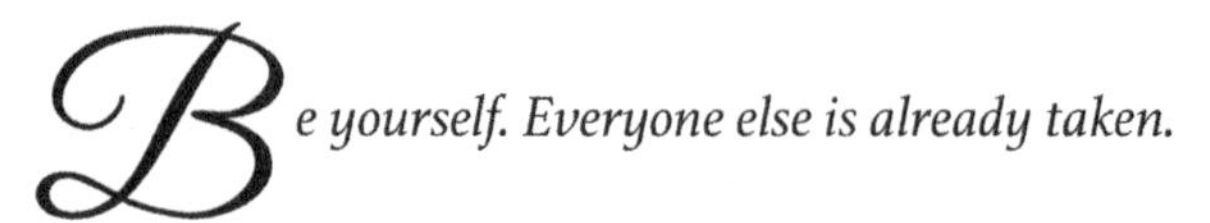

e yourself. Everyone else is already taken.

–Oscar Wilde

LUKE GRABBED her into his arms and held her. She was shaking so hard it was like trying to stand through an earthquake. But she didn't think all the trembling was coming from her. Luke held her hard against him, his heart banging against hers. "You okay?"

She laughed weakly. "My hair's a mess, my dress is ruined and my makeup is a disaster."

She kissed him, blood, soap and all. "But I'm alive."

Frank Henderson stepped forward carefully, sliding once and catching his balance. "We're going to need to ask you a few questions."

"Later," Luke said. "We'll let her clean up first and see her daughter."

A look passed between them and Henderson nodded and

went back to huddle with the rest of the cops, security guards and the housekeeper who'd led them to her.

"Thanks," she said to the woman, touching her arm, as Luke led her away. They slid on sticky ribbons of soap a few times. It was like the first time she'd gone skating, hanging onto her partner for dear life.

"What is this stuff?"

"Laundry soap."

"Good one."

Luke led her back to the service elevator. She had as much enthusiasm about getting into that elevator again as a horse being pushed toward a burning barn.

"It's okay," he said. "I'm right here."

She licked her lips and tasted soap. "I know it must seem crazy for me to get scared now, but—" She was shaking so hard her teeth were chattering.

"Perfectly normal," he said. "It's reaction setting in."

"I don't—"

"Your options are this service elevator, climbing twenty flights of stairs, or going out front to the regular elevators."

Clinging to his arm, she stepped into the service elevator and tried not to freak out when the gate closed and it started to lurch upward.

His arm tightened around her and she concentrated only on that. The strength of his muscles, the heat from his body, the knowledge that he was here and they were fine. Everything else she forced away from her mind. Later she'd think about the horror of the evening. Not now.

"Almost there," he said after a while. "It's going to jerk when it stops."

Then the gate opened and he hustled her out of the service door and down the corridor to her room.

"The key—" she said stupidly as they approached her door. She'd left it—somewhere.

"Got it."

"Toni? Mom!" The two greatest women in the world were running toward her down the corridor.

"Don't hug me, I'm a mess," she protested. But they both flung themselves on her, and the three of them were hugging and crying together.

"You're okay?"

"I'm fine."

"Is that blood?"

"Most of it's not mine."

Linda touched her side and she winced. "A little cut. It's nothing."

"I'll fix her up, Linda," Luke said. "I'm first aid certified."

Linda looked at him, long and steady. Then she turned to her daughter. "You get some sleep, honey. We're right down the hall if you need us."

"Thanks, Mama. I love you guys." She hugged them both again.

"Love you, too, Mom. You won a ring."

"I'll collect it tomorrow."

"The soap's drying," Linda said. "You better get in there and wash off. And let the detective look at that cut."

And then her room door was open and she and Luke were stumbling inside. He held on to her all the way into the bathroom, where he jerked on the shower and let it run hot while he undressed her. Except that the thick, industrial soap glued the fabric of her dress with all its diamonds to her skin. He tried to drag it off but when it caught, she moaned.

"I'm usually smoother at this," he assured her.

She kicked off her shoes and then wished she wasn't such a fervent rule follower when she found her soapy nylons had turned her legs into glue sticks.

Her skin was starting to itch and at this point she could see only one solution. She stepped into the shower, clothes and all.

The pounding spray took all the hardness of the soap away but it also turned her into a slick, sliding, soapy mess. "Watch out," said Luke, holding her when she started to slip.

She tilted her head back and let the water keep washing over her. He still kept a hand on her and when she felt that the worst of the soap slick was washed away, she took his tie in her hand—a blue one with a really bad squiggle pattern—and pulled on it, dragging him toward her. "That soap isn't coming off you, either."

He dragged off his jacket, let it fall to the white tiled floor and then kicked off his own shoes and got in with her.

It still wasn't an easy task to get their clothes off, but it was a lot simpler once the soap was washed out of them.

Even though it seemed counter-intuitive, she took the bar of soap the hotel provided—and to heck with her three-step cleansing routine for once in her life, a little soap wasn't going to kill her. She scrubbed her face, washed her body, and then passed him the bar.

"How's the cut?"

"The scratch has already stopped bleeding."

He touched it. "I can't believe it's not deeper."

"Know what saved me? My diamonds. The bodice was so stiff in order to hold all the diamonds that it was like armor."

He chuckled, and touched her cheek. "I heard they were a girl's best friend."

He was staring at her with a distinctly un-policelike expression in his eyes.

"Aren't you on duty?"

"Dinner break," he snapped, pulling her against him. She looked up into his eyes, ringed with spiky wet lashes and suddenly laughed.

"What?"

"You have done what no other man has done in twenty years," she told him.

"What's that?" his voice was soft, sexy.

"Seen me without a smidge of makeup on."

His hand came up and traced a water droplet down her nose. "I like what I see," he said, and then, leaning forward, kissed her.

~

THANK you for reading Frosted Shadow. The fun continues as Toni keeps on selling makeup and sleuthing with Linda, Tiffany and Luke in Ultimate Concealer.

A Note from Nancy

Dear Reader,

Thank you for reading *Frosted Shadow*. I am so grateful for all the enthusiasm the *Toni Diamond Mysteries* has received.

I hope you'll consider leaving a review and please tell your friends who like cozy mysteries.

Review on Amazon, Goodreads or BookBub.

Don't let the fun end. Let's stay in touch.

Join my newsletter to hear about my new releases and enjoy prizes and bonus content like the Vampire Knitting Club's free prequel, *Tangles and Treasons*, the exciting tale of how the gorgeous Rafe Crosyer was turned into a vampire.

I hope to see you in my private Facebook Group Nancy Warren's Knitwits where the fun continues daily.

Until next time,
Happy Reading,

Nancy

ALSO BY NANCY WARREN

The best way to keep up with new releases, plus enjoy bonus content and prizes is to join Nancy's newsletter at nancywarren.net or her Facebook group www.facebook.com/groups/NancyWarrenKnitwits

Toni Diamond Mysteries

Toni is a successful saleswoman for Lady Bianca Cosmetics in this series of humorous cozy mysteries. Along with having an eye for beauty and a head for business, Toni's got a nose for trouble and she's never shy about following her instincts, even when they lead to murder.

Frosted Shadow - Book 1

Ultimate Concealer - Book 2

Midnight Shimmer - Book 3

A Diamond Choker For Christmas - A Toni Diamond Mysteries Novella

Vampire Knitting Club

Tangles and Treasons - a free prequel for Nancy's newsletter subscribers

The Vampire Knitting Club - Book 1

Stitches and Witches - Book 2

Crochet and Cauldrons - Book 3

Stockings and Spells - Book 4

Purls and Potions - Book 5

Fair Isle and Fortunes - Book 6

Lace and Lies - Book 7

Bobbles and Broomsticks - Book 8

Popcorn and Poltergeists - Book 9

Garters and Gargoyles - Book 10

Diamonds and Daggers - Book 11

Cat's Paws and Curses a Holiday Whodunnit

Vampire Knitting Club Boxed Set 1-3

The Vampire Book Club

The Vampire Book Club - Book 1

Chapter and Curse - Book 2

A Spelling Mistake - Book 3

The Great Witches Baking Show

The Great Witches Baking Show - Book 1

Baker's Coven - Book 2

A Rolling Scone - Book 3

A Bundt Instrument - Book 4

Blood, Sweat and Tiers - Book 5

Abigail Dixon Historical Mystery

Death of a Flapper - In 1920s Paris everything is très chic, except murder.

The Almost Wives Club

An enchanted wedding dress is a matchmaker in this series of romantic comedies where five runaway brides find out who the best men really are!

The Almost Wives Club: Kate - Book 1

Second Hand Bride - Book 2

Bridesmaid for Hire - Book 3

The Wedding Flight - Book 4

If the Dress Fits - Book 5

Take a Chance series

Meet the Chance family, a cobbled together family of eleven kids who are all grown up and finding their ways in life and love.

Kiss a Girl in the Rain - Book 1

Iris in Bloom - Book 2

Blueprint for a Kiss - Book 3

Every Rose - Book 4

Love to Go - Book 5

The Sheriff's Sweet Surrender - Book 6

The Daisy Game - Book 7

Chance Encounter - Prequel

Take a Chance Box Set - Prequel and Books 1-3

For a complete list of books, check out Nancy's website at nancywarren.net

ABOUT THE AUTHOR

Nancy Warren is the USA Today Bestselling author of more than 70 novels. She's originally from Vancouver, Canada, though she tends to wander and has lived in England, Italy and California at various times. Favorite moments include being the answer to a crossword puzzle clue in Canada's National Post newspaper, being featured on the front page of the New York Times when her book Speed Dating launched Harlequin's NASCAR series, and being nominated three times for Romance Writers of America's RITA award. She has an MA in Creative Writing from Bath Spa University. She's an avid hiker, loves chocolate and most of all, loves to hear from readers! The best way to stay in touch is to sign up for Nancy's newsletter at www.nancywarren.net.

To learn more about Nancy and her books

www.nancywarren.net